DELPHINE
AND THE
SILVER NEEDLE

DELPHINE
AND THE
SILVER NEEDLE

ALYSSA MOON

DISNEP • HYPERION
LOS ANGELES   NEW YORK

First Edition, March 2021
10 9 8 7 6 5 4 3 2 1
FAC-020093-20234
Printed in the United States of America

Designed by Marci Senders

This book is set in Baskerville MT Pro/Monotype; Caslon Antique/Monotype; Copperplate Gothic LT Pro/Monotype; Elaina Script/Fontspring; Isabel Unicase/Fontspring

Library of Congress Cataloging-in-Publication Data

Names: Moon, Alyssa, author.
Title: Delphine and the silver needle / Alyssa Moon.
Description: First edition. • Los Angeles : Disney Hyperion, 2021. •
    Series: Delphine • Audience: Ages 8–12. • Audience: Grades 4–6. •
    Summary: When sixteen-year-old Delphine, a dressmaker mouse in
    Cinderella's chateau, learns of her connection to the Threaded, magical
    tailor mice of legend, she undertakes an epic quest to claim her
    identity.
Identifiers: LCCN 2020002245 • ISBN 9781368048026 (hardcover) •
    ISBN 9781368056519 (ebook)
Subjects: CYAC: Adventure and adventurers—Fiction. • Mice—Fiction. •
    Magic—Fiction. • Tailors—Fiction. • Identity—Fiction. •
    Foundlings—Fiction. • Fairy tales.
Classification: LCC PZ8.M787 Del 2020 • DDC [Fic]—dc23
LC record available at https://lccn.loc.gov/2020002245

Reinforced binding

Visit www.DisneyBooks.com

For my grandmother, Jane Elizabeth

Prologue

Deep in the Kingdom of Peltinore, puddles of moonlight glowed on the cobblestones and lay across the shuttered windows of the Château Desjardins. In the barn, sheep and horses dozed. Everything was quiet except for the hooting of an owl in the forest nearby.

On the main doorstep, all was still. And on the little mouse-size doorstep next to it, a shimmer hung in the air, just as it always had. Then, without warning, buzzing wisps of light began to gather. The wisps swirled and joined in a sudden burst of magic so dazzling that the whole front of the house shone bright as day. In another instant, the flash was gone, taking the odd shimmer along with it. The puddle of moonlight remained, though it no longer lay on an empty stoop. Now it illuminated a tiny bundle.

After a while, dawn crept over the horizon. The residents of the château began to stir, human and mouse alike. Toes touched cold flagstones and were pulled back into bed for a few more moments. A human mother lifted her baby from the crib and kissed her forehead.

In one of the tiny homes hidden in the wall alongside the human stairs, the mouse Meline tightened her apron strings and brushed her ears back under a sensible work cap. Picking up her broom, she unlatched her front door into the passageway. It was her turn to sweep the little mouse doorstep of the château. Some of the other mice shirked this task, unwilling to admit they were afraid of the odd shimmer that hung in the air. Meline sniffed at this attitude. That shimmer had always been there, no different from the dust motes that danced through sunbeams in the barn. No mouse of Château Desjardins could remember a time when the front doorstep had ever been without the odd glimmer, so why be afraid?

The air was crisp as the old front door swung open under her paw. Gazing up at the first leaves beginning to change color, it took Meline a moment to notice the package on the little doorstep. A bundle of linens? Rags left by a wandering peddler? She could see an oversize human needle had been woven in and out through the fabric on one side of the bundle. Odd.

Meline stepped closer, suddenly noticing that the strange glimmer in the air was gone. Her heart caught in her throat. What had happened? Just then, a tiny squeak sounded from within the bundle. All other thoughts disappeared as Meline knelt to snatch up the linens, realizing what was inside:

A baby mouse, a little girl, no more than a few months old.

Meline rested her paw on the baby's cheek, and the little one gazed up at Meline, wide-eyed and serious. Then she sneezed. Her fur was the color of early-morning fog, and she had strange gray whiskers, the likes of which Meline had never seen.

"You're safe now," Meline whispered. "You're mine, and I'm yours." Leaving her broom forgotten on the doorstep (most unlike Meline!), she carried the baby inside to spread word of the incredible arrival.

tHe Brie m●●n

Chapter 1

Delphine rolled over and buried her head under her pillow. The morning sun was streaming through her window, tickling her whiskers and calling for her to awaken, but she had stayed up too late again, sewing by the light of one of the candle ends in her workshop.

It never failed. Whenever Delphine started a new project, she lost track of time. She would sew and sew, until invariably her mother came yawning down the corridor to remind her it was time for bed. So when her mother had shown up last night, as always, Delphine had set aside her scraps of fabric in one of the many walnut shells she used to store her projects and tiptoed back down the curving hallways toward her home under the human stairs.

Now she tried to snuggle deeper into her thistledown bed, tucking her tail under the covers where it was warm. Maybe she would be able to drift back to sleep. But it was no use. She could hear the old hound, Bruno, barking happily in the yard, which meant Cinderella was already gathering eggs from the hen coop. And if Cinderella was up, then Delphine could manage to drag herself out of bed as well.

She splashed a quick bit of water on her face and smoothed back her gray whiskers, peering into the chip of mirror leaning against the wall behind her ewer and basin. *Such dull gray whiskers*, she thought for the thousandth time. *None of the other Desjardins mice have gray whiskers. Why must I?* But she knew the answer. Because as much as she *was* a Desjardins mouse, ever since the day she had been found on the little doorstep, she hadn't been *born* a Desjardins mouse. She had no idea where she had come from; she only knew the story her mother had told so many times.

Delphine glanced up at the oversize human needle that had arrived with her that fateful day. It had hung in that spot on the wall since the morning her new mother had brought her into the room sixteen years earlier.

"I laid you down into a makeshift crib," Meline always said fondly. "You were so tiny, I had to use the shell of a hazelnut. Can you imagine?" And as a youngling, Delphine had always giggled, imagining herself being that small.

"I tucked you in with the blanket from my bed," her mother would continue, "and you fell fast asleep in an instant. The linens that you had been swaddled in, and the huge needle—that was all you had with you. I folded the linens around the needle, and I hung it on the wall just above your cradle so that you could see it. I thought it should stay close."

And so Delphine had grown up with the needle in view every night of her life. Many times she had climbed up onto her bed to run her paws along the needle's dark tarnished surface, wondering what mysteries it held. Why a *human* needle? And what were the strange engravings along the shaft, looking almost as if they had been born out of the clouded silver surface itself? The linens, too, and that strange crest that was embroidered onto them—nobody had ever been able to tell her what it meant.

"Delphine!" Maman called now, interrupting her thoughts. "Breakfast!"

Delphine threw on her overskirt and apron, hastily knotted a fichu around her shoulders, and scampered down the hall.

The kitchen windows were already steamy from the pot of dandelion soup bubbling on the stovetop. Fresh brioche crumbs sat heating in the little ember-oven. *Brioche!* Delphine had forgotten it was Friday. She cringed.

Maman stood at the kitchen countertop, flour on her paws and snout, kneading dough for the evening tartelette. She was as beautiful as always, with gentle ridges of cream and brown fur across her cheeks, broad country ears, and sweeping chestnut whiskers.

"Morning, Maman," said Delphine quickly, taking down two button-plates from the cupboard. She served up a dollop of fresh, rich butter onto each. Her mother pulled open the door of the ember-oven and whisked out the crumbs with a swift flick of the paw, placing them onto the plates.

"You know, Delphine," said Maman gently, "the best crumbs always go to whoever gets to the human kitchen first on Friday mornings." She wiped her paws on the corner of a mouse-size tea cloth, a scrap from an old human towel.

That was Maman's subtle way of reminding Delphine that crumb duty had been *her* responsibility, and she had slept right through it.

Delphine sighed, twisting her peculiar gray whiskers around one paw. "I didn't *mean* to sleep in."

Maman sat down on the bench made of folded human playing cards. "I know you didn't, darling. But you stay up so late sewing away that your chores are starting to be affected. Dreams are important, but don't forget about your responsibilities in the real world."

Delphine sat down next to her mother and they began their

breakfast. She thought of all the other Desjardins mice living in the nooks and crannies of the château, sitting down to breakfast at the same time before heading to their daily jobs. It had been the same ever since she could remember.

They nibbled at the hot, fragrant brioche crumbs. Delphine sighed. She had been so busy lately, she hadn't even had time to see her friends Gus and Jaq, hadn't participated in any of the summer's-end festivities. And now summer was over.

"Maman!" she said suddenly. "What if we just skipped our jobs today, and went for a snail ride instead?" She could already feel the fresh air in her whiskers, the leather reins in her paws, the slow, steady pace of the snails.

Her mother smiled good-naturedly. "And leave the little pinkie mice without onesies to wear? Who will help sew those if you aren't at your spot in the row?"

Delphine wrinkled her nose and crammed the rest of the brioche into her mouth. "It's the most tedious thing. They won't let me make up my own designs, or add any interesting details, or try anything new."

"That's why you have your workshop, so that you can sew whatever you like in the evenings." Her mother rose, clearing the table. "Until a reasonable hour, of course," she added.

Delphine leaned on the counter, watching her rinse off the plates in the stone washtub. "But you love my gowns."

Her mother laughed. "We all do, sweet pea! They're

beautiful. But they're fit for a royal ball, not everyday wear. Why do you think your aunt Roselle borrowed one for her visit to the palace last month?"

"Because she liked it," Delphine muttered.

"Because she *loved* it," corrected her mother. "So keep sewing. But that means during the day for the pinkie mice as well. We must find a balance, chérie."

Delphine finished wiping off the table and retied her apron. Her mother peered into the tiny shard of mirror hanging on the wall, adjusting her bonnet to cover her ears. Then she turned.

"Now, before we head off to work . . . I have something for you. A human messenger arrived from the castle with an announcement for the Desjardins girls early this morning. There's to be a ball, and all the humans are invited. Though that's not the real news. A mouse messenger also came along to deliver *this*!"

Maman drew something from her apron pocket, a creamy envelope of thick linen paper. She held it out to Delphine with a curious expression. "Have you been sending letters to the castle?"

"N-no . . ." stammered Delphine. She took it with trembling paws.

A gold wax seal on the envelope flap featured the mouse princess's crest: a thick slice of Camembert cheese above two crossed wheat sheaves. On the other side was her very own name, written in ornate copperplate:

Mademoiselle Delphine Desjardins

Delphine gasped. The residents of Château Desjardins almost never received communication from the court, and certainly never personal correspondence. Delphine cracked open the wax seal and carefully pulled out the card. It, too, was made of the same fine linen paper and was delicately lettered with the same copperplate, words interlinking in luxurious swoops of gold ink that danced across the page.

The presence of Mademoiselle Delphine Desjardins
is requested tomorrow
to provide dressmaking services
to Princess Petits-Oiseaux
at the stroke of twelve noon by the castle clock

Delphine's mouth fell open. "I'm going to the castle?"

Maman was reading over her shoulder. She stared back at Delphine with delight. "My very own daughter, summoned to sew for the princess?" She swept Delphine into her arms, glowing with pride.

Delphine's head was spinning. "But how . . . ?"

Her mother shook her head slowly, uncertain. "When Roselle wore your gown there for her last visit . . . could the princess have seen it?" She ran a paw along Delphine's whiskers. "Your clothes are one of a kind. It would have been impossible to miss.

In any case, you can take the vegetable farmer's cart first thing in the morning." She glanced out the window. "But we'd better get going now. We both still have a full day's work ahead of us before tomorrow."

Delphine jumped up, overflowing with excitement. She didn't think she could possibly go about her chores with something so extraordinary on the horizon. And yet the day flew by in the blink of an eye; before she knew it, dinner and the tartelette had already come and gone. As the sun began to set through the tall oak trees outside of the château windows, Delphine scurried through the passages for nursery duty. The little orphan mice sat waiting for her with their nurse keeping watch. Delphine settled down on a mound of pillows in the middle of the room as the tots crowded close.

"Once upon a time," she began, snuggling all the little mice up around her, "there lived the Threaded, right here in this very kingdom." This was one of Delphine's favorite fairy tales. She herself had asked to hear it over and over when she was young, and now she delighted in sharing it with the newest members of the Desjardins clan. It also made nursery duty her favorite of the château chores. "The Threaded," she went on, "were magical mice who were not only the best seamstresses and tailors in the land, but could even perform *magical* sewing with their needles."

"What's magical sewing?" piped up one of the little ones, wide-eyed.

"Nobody really knows," she replied, "but I like to think

that they embroidered butterflies whose wings could flutter, and roses that smelled like real roses plucked fresh from the rosebush."

The toddler mice *ooh*ed in wonder at the idea.

"Now, the Threaded," Delphine continued, "sewed for all of the noblemice of our kingdom. They were here for hundreds of years in Peltinore, passing down their magic, generation after generation. And there were always twelve of them. No more, and no less. Do you remember the rhyme?"

They recited along with her:

The First rides the wind. The Second walks on light.
The Third bends the waves. The Fourth moves with might.
The Fifth sings with birds. The Sixth paints the sky.
The Seventh writes the song. The Eighth draws the eye.
The Ninth touches stars. The Tenth sweetens tart.
The Eleventh reads the dreams. And the Twelfth knows the heart.

"That's right!" Delphine said, delighted. "You know the rhyme even better than I do."

"What happened to the Threaded?" the littlest mouse asked.

Delphine sighed. "They disappeared. Nobody knows where they went, or why. But some say that one day they'll return, and we'll have magical mice in our midst once more."

The little mouse cheered, rocking on her rear paws.

"Is magic real?" said another toddler mouse.

"As real as you want it to be," said Delphine, smiling. "And now it's time for bed." She picked them up one by one, carrying them gently to their cribs lined up along the sides of the room. As she tucked them in, she sang an ancient mouse lullaby: *"Whiskers soft and eyes are closed. Time for baby mine to doze."* After she had tucked the last one beneath his covers, Delphine quietly blew out the candle end and tiptoed out of the room.

As she passed through the château walls, she could hear Lady Tremaine arguing yet again with her two daughters. She was castigating them for forgetting to reset the mousetraps. Delphine shivered. Cinderella always sprang the traps whenever she found them in the château, out of kindness to the mice. But it made Delphine's blood run cold to hear the lady of the house speak so cruelly.

With Lady Tremaine's voice still ringing in her ears, she entered the little nook that served as her workshop. It was built inside a wall cornice, with funny angles and corners. But to Delphine, it was the best room in the château, especially because Cinderella did her mending and sewing in the parlor directly below. It felt almost as if they were sitting and sewing together . . . even if Cinderella didn't know it. Delphine had learned all her best sewing techniques that way, studying from above.

As usual, Delphine's workshop was a disaster. There were piles of leftover fabric trimmings from human gowns, thimbles full of seed beads spilling onto the floor, and half-finished projects hanging from every rafter. She glanced down through the little window into the parlor to see if Cinderella was in her usual spot.

Alas, there was not a human in sight, only Lucifer sharpening his claws on the good sofa. Mean old cat. The château would have been far more pleasant without him—or the other cruel residents—in it. Delphine sighed and turned back to the task at hand. She needed to put her best paw forward if she was going to make a good impression at the castle tomorrow.

First things first, she thought. *I'll need a measuring tape.* She dug through pile after pile, tossing fabric and thread here and there, but couldn't find a single one. Delphine groaned. Now that she had a chance to think about it, the trip to the castle felt daunting. How could she make a dress for the princess if she couldn't even take her measurements? Then Delphine began to realize that she had no idea what Princess Petits-Oiseaux was actually expecting of her. Could she even deliver to the princess's standards? What *were* the standards of dressmaking for a princess? Delphine's tail twitched nervously.

Taking a deep breath, she decided to distract herself by gathering other items from the piles that might be useful—a lacquer pin box, her lucky pair of scissors, a basket that seemed nice enough to carry everything to the castle. A measuring tape eventually turned up underneath the human thimble that she used as a hat stand.

Still feeling butterflies whirling in her stomach—and not

the magical, embroidered kind she'd described to the mice babies earlier—Delphine left her workshop. On an impulse, she turned and climbed the steep flight of stairs inside the wall up to Cinderella's tower room. She scurried to the ledge of the window and gazed at the giant castle's elegant towers on the horizon. They glimmered in the evening starlight. This was what she'd always wanted, she reminded herself. A change in the doldrums of château life! A chance to sew something truly special! An adventure, if only for a day! She reached down with a tentative paw to be sure the invitation was still in her pocket. She could feel the shape of the envelope through the starchy fabric of her apron.

Besides, Delphine had dreamt of visiting the castle ever since she could remember, and opportunities to travel there were few and far between. Delphine had practically given up hope that she would ever get the chance. And now, not only was she headed there, she was going to meet the princess!

Delphine took another deep breath to steady herself.

Magic may not be real, she thought, *but tomorrow will be magical.*

Chapter 2

The next morning, a loud chirping broke the stillness. Delphine blinked drowsily to see her friends Cittine and Margeaux, two of the château sparrows, poking their heads through her window. The sky behind them was still dark.

"You said to wake you early!" trilled Margeaux.

"So here we are!" chimed in Cittine. They fluttered up to Cinderella's tower window. Delphine watched them go, wishing for the thousandth time that she could fly. Seeing the world from high above . . . it would be incredible. If only she could ask them for a ride, but the code between animals would never permit that.

She scrambled into her nicest clothes, tucked a clean handkerchief into her apron pocket, and grabbed her basket of supplies. *The envelope!* She had almost forgotten it on her dressing table. Doubling back, she carefully tucked it into her pocket, then scurried down the stairs inside the wall. There was no time to waste if she was going to catch a ride on the vegetable farmer's cart. In the human kitchen at the end of the passage ahead, she could already hear Cinderella singing softly.

The crunch of wheels on the gravel grabbed Delphine's attention. She ran across the front parlor, praying that Lucifer was still asleep. There was no time to go through the circuitous corridors in the walls.

As soon as Delphine scampered outside, she looked around. There stood the vegetable farmer's cart, the farmer climbing back aboard into his seat. She had gotten there just in time! Hiking up her skirts, she hurried across the gravel, leaping from one stone to the next. She could see the farmer picking up the reins and the dappled horse stepping in place gently. Delphine leapt into a flat-out dash across the remaining distance and scampered up the side of the cart just as it began to move. The jouncing of all four wheels over the uneven road jostled and tumbled her around the back of the cart. She waved at the château, picturing the mouse residents still tucked into their beds, until the cart turned and her home disappeared from sight.

It was official: Delphine was heading to the castle for the first time.

Now she just had to follow her mother's instructions about how and where to switch conveyances. *It's a pity that humans never travel from Château Desjardins straight to the castle*, she mused, watching the fields pass by and the sun begin to rise. The air was sweet with the fragrance of wheat being harvested, and bumblebees paused from time to time to rest on the cart as it bounced along the winding road.

Delphine disembarked at the crossroads where all the human drivers stopped to water their horses. Her mother had said she'd have to wait there for another cart to take her the rest of the way. Around her, little knots of mice stood gossiping, watching the coaches and carts being unloaded and refilled with both human and mouse parcels. Delivery mice darted to and fro with bags of goods slung across their shoulders. One had an ingenious sort of wheelbarrow with an extra-wide wheel that could surmount even the largest pebbles. The wheel was made from an empty thread spool, Delphine realized with admiration. A few gophers and voles skittered through the crowds, clearly running their own errands.

Delphine hung back, not sure whom to approach for information. Each animal seemed busier than the last. Then she spotted an elderly florist mouse named Clothilde that she knew from the Sunday markets along the country road by the château. She and her mother had been buying flowers from Clothilde ever since Delphine could remember. She felt certain that the mouse could help her figure out which transport to take.

Delphine approached and sat down beside Clothilde on a long bench made from a discarded human pitchfork handle. Other hopeful travelers perched on either side of them, all headed to their own destinations. The long grass behind the bench swayed gently in the morning breeze, bringing the smell of roasted acorns to Delphine's nose. It seemed someone had decided to prepare an early snack while they waited, and Delphine wished she had had the forethought to have done the same.

"Bonjour, Madame Clothilde," Delphine said, doing her best to act grown-up and at ease. She wrapped her tail demurely around her ankles under her petticoats.

Clothilde nodded at Delphine with a wink, her bright old eyes just visible beneath the brim of her wide wicker hat. She clasped a huge basket in her paws.

"Bonjour, my dear. I've never seen you at the crossroads. Where are you headed today? Off to a grand adventure?"

"I'm going to the castle." Delphine tried to sound noncha-lant, but she was starting to feel overwhelmed once more with all the uncertainty that lay before her. She smoothed down her whiskers.

Clothilde gently took Delphine's paw. "The castle is a place of wonder," she said. "Dreams can come true within those walls. I will never forget my first visit. And neither will you." She leaned forward, casting her gaze across the group of human coaches and carts pulled up around the watering trough. "The baker is, I think, heading there. As is the chirurgeon. You'll be able to ride with whichever is the next to leave."

She glanced back at Delphine, another smile tugging at the corners of her eyes, and continued. "Enjoy every moment, curtsey to all the noblemice, and compliment Princess Petits-Oiseaux on her curlicue whisker. It rests on the leftmost side of her muzzle, and she is extremely proud of it. The other ladymice of the court often wear one whisker curled in imitation of hers." Clothilde wrapped one of Delphine's gray whiskers around her paw in jovial demonstration.

Delphine's eyes grew wide. "Mouse whiskers can be curled?" She had never even considered this possibility.

Clothilde smiled. "All things are possible at the castle."

Just then, the human baker clambered onto the seat of her cart, gathering her reins. The giant roan horse tossed its head in response.

"The baker's cart it is!" said Clothilde, pointing. "Be quick, before it pulls away!"

"Thank you, Madame Clothilde!" Delphine grabbed up her basket, then turned and ran toward the rumbling cart.

Luckily, Delphine was fast. She dashed alongside the horse, squeaking a quick "Bonjour!" as she passed. The horse cast its slow view downward and flared its nostrils in clear disinterest. Delphine reached the side of the cart and leapt nimbly onto a piece of trailing rope. Shinnying onto the back of the driver's box, she squeezed herself in with the other animal passengers. The gruff old shrew next to her barely glanced her way before returning his gaze to the road winding beneath the cart.

Delphine leaned back to catch her breath, watching the Chanterelle River running past them. It cut through the middle of this little part of the kingdom and flowed out to sea. Perched atop the cart, she could see sunlight sparkling like jewels on the surface of the river.

The cart jostled over bridges, rocking the passengers, but Delphine didn't mind. She could smell the fresh baguettes loaded in the back, and the sunshine warmed her.

They passed through Leyzizes, where her mother headed whenever Delphine needed new wire ends for needles and pins. They hurtled past a clear blue lake and through Chaumont so quickly that Delphine didn't even have time to look for the famous lizard fiddlers who were said to play on top of the city square arbor. There was so much to see that it made Delphine's head spin.

Then, after what seemed like forever, the cart began to climb upward. The incline grew steeper and steeper. She heard the horses whuffle and raised her eyes to see why. Her breath caught in her throat.

The castle—closer than she had ever been before.

It appeared tower by tower over the hilltop as the horses raced forward. Spires sprouted atop every roof and cornice, displaying flags with the royal crest of the human king. Panels of yellow and pink glass sparkled around the edges of windows, the latter matching the stones that capped the guardhouses of the outer wall. The turrets almost glowed; it seemed as if the clouds themselves were reaching down to reflect that golden light.

"We're nearly there!" squealed Delphine, hugging herself. Her tail lashed excitedly, hitting the legs of the elderly shrew beside her.

He peered at her from beneath his brows. "I am aware, young lady," he harrumphed. "And I would appreciate it if you and your tail could both remain in control of yourselves until we arrive."

Delphine grabbed at her tail with both paws, fumbling to get it tucked back under her skirts. Her cheeks flamed. *If that were to happen at court!* she thought.

The cart slowed to a crawl as it passed over the moat and approached a side gate. Human guards waved the baker through, and she tipped her cap as she passed, nudging her horses through the narrow opening in the wall and into a short stone passage. More human guards approached the cart as they came to a stop, this time apparently to check the cargo.

Delphine stared in awe at what lay ahead. The passage led toward a massive interior courtyard ringed by stables. The sheer number of carts, coaches, humans, horses, chickens, and general bedlam contained in the open space ahead of her was enough to make Delphine light-headed.

"Everyone off!" piped a shrill voice, and a young mouse in a scarlet doublet came scurrying up the wheel and onto the cart. "Get into the entry hall, where it's safe! You know where to go!"

The rest of the passengers apparently did. They had their satchels gathered and hanging from their travel twigs before Delphine had the chance to even pull her thoughts together.

The mouse ran over to her. "Off, off, before they lead the cart into the stable courtyard! Don't want to be dismounting in there around all those horses' hooves." He gave Delphine a quick shove, and she scrambled over the edge and down the wheel to the flagstones.

The other passengers were disappearing through a narrow gate spanning the crack between two stones in the castle wall. Delphine followed. She emerged from the fissure into a hallway so large, she would have thought it was a human room if she hadn't known better. Small animals ran madly in every direction, each seeming to be on a more important errand than the last. The vaulted stone ceiling echoed every sound back downward on itself, creating a cacophonous din. High on one wall, a sundial was cleverly mounted to catch the sun's rays. It was just a few whisker-lengths from being noon. Delphine had no idea how long it would take to reach the princess's quarters, but if the rest of the mouse portion of the castle was as vast as this room, it might just take her all day.

The mouse who had hurried Delphine into the chamber now turned to a large, swarthy vole in a velvet surcoat and announced, "Baker's just pulled in."

The vole scanned his sheaf of papers. "Team Tyrol, grain duty!" he hollered in no particular direction, and then turned back to his papers, scribbling furiously.

Delphine was suddenly buffeted by a group of long-legged mice running at full speed toward the passage back out to the courtyard.

How did they even hear *him in all this hubbub?* Delphine wondered.

"You always pick on us for grain duty!" retorted the last mouse as she ran past, biting her thumb at the vole. "We're sick of it, *Rat*sus!"

The vole's cheeks puffed in indignation. "You know perfectly well my name is Rassus, you—you weevil!" he snarled back. He flicked his gaze about, and his sights landed on Delphine. "You!" he bellowed.

She drew back.

He narrowed his eyes at her. "What are you doing standing around? Tell one of the valets where you're going, and hurry it up! We're all on a tight schedule!"

Delphine swallowed. "The valets?"

But he had already turned away and was arguing once more, this time with a mouse trying to bring in a massive wooden box containing several chirping crickets.

Delphine spun around. The mouse who had escorted her off the cart had been swallowed up by the crowd, but she could see a few other scarlet-doubleted mice at the far end of the hall. She headed that way, threading between nannies toting pinkie mice, merchants and vendors dragging baskets of wares, and elegant young ladymice and gentlemice strolling undisturbed through the hectic scene. A huddle of them stared at Delphine's frock, giggling behind their fans. Delphine colored and hurried on.

At the far end of the room, she tentatively approached the valet who looked the least harried.

"Yes, yes?" said the valet before Delphine had even caught her breath.

"I'm—" Delphine fished in her pocket for the card. "I'm, um, here to see Princess Petits-Oiseaux?" She gulped, fearing she sounded like a common cabbage herder.

The valet plucked the card from her paw and scanned it, muttering under her breath. "Princess . . . noon . . ." She glanced back up at Delphine. "You need an escort, I assume. First visit to the castle?"

Delphine shrank inside. Was it *that* obvious? She nodded.

The valet handed the card back to her. "Rostreau!" she called to a group of noblemice nearby, standing idly and chatting. "Escort needed!"

A pale mouse with a pleated red cap dangling off one ear

glanced at the valet and waved a gloved paw dismissively. "Oh, Octavie," he drawled back. "Can't you see I'm busy?"

"Rostreau!" she demanded again.

He turned back to the other noblemice, smirking.

The valet's whiskers quivered in anger. "They think they're so special." Her eye caught Delphine's. "That's the castle for you. Everyone's better than someone else. You'll see." She slammed down her papers on a nearby pile of flour sacks, ignoring the resulting puff of flour that rose up in a cloud. Indignantly she stalked off across the busy hall, tail swishing madly, flour now dusting the side of her pants.

Delphine watched Octavie go. Was she supposed to wait? Being late for the princess would make an awful first impression. She smoothed her skirts nervously.

"Bonjour!" came a sudden voice.

Delphine jumped.

A foppish, ruddy-furred mouse with a white chin and neck had stepped out from the crowd in front of her. He looked no older than she but held himself like a pompous king, dressed from head to toe in embroidered emerald velvet. He swooshed his cape from side to side, then bowed so low she thought he was going to try to kiss her toe.

He stood back up, eyebrow cocked, then leaned in convivially. "I hear you are going to see the princess?"

"Uh, y-yes," she stammered. "That's right. I've been asked—"

The noblemouse cut her off. "I would never ask a lady to divulge her private business. I need no reason to escort you other than the pleasure of your company, mademoiselle." He reached for her paw.

She gave it hesitantly, unsure what he was planning until he wrapped it around his arm with a little press. "I—" Delphine tried to look back across the hall for Octavie, but he still had her paw firmly in his grip. She yanked it away. "The valet—"

He did the eyebrow thing again. "No need. You now have the pleasure of the acquaintance of Lord Alexander de Soucy Perrault, of the Poirier Perraults. You *have* heard of me, I'm sure."

She hadn't. But she wasn't about to admit that.

"And you are . . . ?" he prompted.

"I am, uh, Delphine Desjardins."

He coughed politely.

"Of Château Desjardins," she added awkwardly. Was she supposed to say that? She wasn't sure.

"Lady Delphine Desjardins of Château Desjardins, it is my honor to make your most esteemed acquaintance." Another extremely deep bow.

She watched in concern, hoping he would be able to make it back up again without tipping over. But he straightened easily, a brand-new smoldering look plastered across his lips and eyebrows.

Did he think that was attractive?

"Give me the honor of escorting you," the noblemouse

continued. "I shall provide a most enjoyable tour of the castle as we walk." This time, instead of reaching for her paw, he smoothed his whiskers back with an affected twirl of the wrist, obviously hoping to show off the detail of his lace cuff. Which, Delphine had to admit, was impressively intricate.

Delphine glanced at the sundial on the wall. Octavie was still nowhere to be seen.

She sighed.

Be kind, Cinderella always said. Delphine could at least do that.

"Thank you, Lord Perrault de . . . um . . . Soucy," she said. "Please lead the way." She gestured and then fell in step behind him, keeping her paws folded firmly around her basket handle, away from his grasp.

Chapter 3

Lord Alexander de Soucy Perrault led Delphine through the winding hallways and staircases of the mouse castle. She could see how cunningly the passages and rooms had been built into the walls of the human castle, just like the passages inside the halls of Château Desjardins. As they walked, the lord plied her with anecdotes of his bravery, cutting ripostes, and knowledge of romantic poetry. At least he pointed out some interesting sights, but she wished he would walk at a quicker pace. It had to be nearly noon.

"Those stairs lead to the bell tower of the castle," Lord Perrault said, gesturing to a winding staircase. "That is where the astrologers chart the fortunes of the noblemice." Then he smiled winningly. "The lead astrologer is a vole of great age and wisdom, and I am in her good graces. Perhaps one day I shall introduce you to her for your own fortune to be read."

Delphine wasn't sure how to respond. "How kind," she finally said.

They passed the mouse bakery, with its ovens built into the bricks of a human chimney. "The cold cooks are all in the rear kitchens," Lord Perrault explained, "along with all the grain preparation. The baked goods are prepared here and then brought to the main kitchen to be assembled." That seemed exceedingly confusing to Delphine, but everything about the castle was starting to make her head spin. It was a maze of passages, all leading up, down, and sideways.

As they crossed through one main intersection, she paused before an ominous-looking arch in the wall with guards posted on either side. "What's that?"

Lord Perrault stopped and glanced back. "The entrance to the Forbidden Wing," he said. "It was abandoned over a century ago, after the War to End All Wars. Not much to see there. Now, shouldn't we be hurrying?"

Delphine nearly laughed at his question. Of *course* they should be hurrying. But she merely nodded.

"Now, up ahead," he continued, "you'll see my favorite painting of our first king and queen, rest their paws and whiskers." He paused next to a small painting on a disk of ivory. "I like to think that I resemble His Royal Highness in the snout and ears." He puffed out his chest and turned his head sideways.

She glanced briefly at the painting and then continued a few steps onward, hoping she could encourage him to hurry without causing offense. "Fascinating, Lord Perrault de Soucy," she called back to him.

"There's no need to be so formal!" He raced to catch up with her. "Call me Alexander, I beseech you."

She nodded. Court manners were entirely foreign to her, but that certainly was less of a mouthful.

Alexander launched into another tale of single-handedly fending off a whole band of hawkworms that had been plotting to overtake the castle gardens. "I parried as if driven by lightning!" he cried, dancing to and fro in the hallway as he acted out the fight.

She groaned inwardly. Given how clean and perfect Alexander's garments were, she could guess that he spent much more of his time inside, playing cards with his lordly friends, than outdoors in any gardens or stopping unwanted invasions.

The hallway made a gentle curve and then another.

Will we ever reach the princess's quarters? Delphine wondered.

Another lord mouse came toward them, his golden velvet slippers flopping fashionably at the heels. He bowed low to Alexander, who bowed even lower in return. Then he glanced sideways at Delphine.

"Lord Ponceroy de Clairemonde Villeneuve, charmed to make your acquaintance," he drawled obsequiously. He turned back to Alexander. "Listen, you old gnat, we're going down to the village tonight for some, ah . . ." He gazed at Delphine again and then turned his snout away, mouthing the word *cards* to Alexander under his breath. "Coming along? Clarenton says he'll provide common togs again for us to wear." He dabbed at his brow with a gold-embroidered handkerchief, an obvious affectation.

Alexander's whiskers had the grace to twitch at the reference to "common togs" in front of Delphine. "Can't," he said. "I have rather more important plans." He bowed low, then took Delphine's elbow and steered her around Lord Ponceroy de Clairemonde.

"Adieu!" Ponceroy called snidely from behind them. "And to *you*, kind lady whomever-you-are!" Then she could hear him traipsing on down the corridor, his slippers flapping against the ground once more.

Delphine snuck a glance at Alexander. "You go to the village?"

"What? No! Well, ah, sometimes." He actually seemed at a loss for words, the first time since they'd met. But in a split second, he had already regained his composure. "'Tis an enjoy-able way to make merry with the everyday folk of the kingdom," he said suavely.

Cleverly answered, thought Delphine. But it sounded a lot to her as if the nobles played at being poor, just for fun. Life in the castle wasn't what she had expected at all.

Alexander continued babbling as they walked. Only when he stopped midsentence did she realize they were standing before a set of grand stone doors, covered with delicate carvings of snowdrops. A guard was positioned on either side of the doors, their spears crossed.

"Oh. Well, would you look at that? We're here!" He pulled off his cap with a grand swoosh. "My lady?"

She grimaced, then realized too late he had interpreted this as an enthusiastic smile.

"I shall await your return!" he said delightedly.

"No need," she blurted. "I'm sure the guards here can summon another escort. I wouldn't want for you to waste your valuable time waiting, good sir."

But Alexander dismissed the idea with a flick of his wrist. "Absurd. I shall be here, looking forward to further time spent in your charming presence." He turned and sauntered away to the end of the hall, his cape tossed back over his shoulder with a little too much care to be accidental.

One guard pulled back his spear and thrust out a paw. Of course—the card. Delphine pulled it out again, and the guard examined it, staring closely at the royal seal. The other guard kept her spear firmly across the door, eyeballing Delphine through the slit in her gleaming iron helmet.

"Wait here." The first guard disappeared through the doors, leaving Delphine standing awkwardly in the hallway. She gazed down at her dress, away from the other guard's piercing stare. What would she say to the princess?

"I'm a seamstress," she whispered. She almost choked on the word.

Princess Petits-Oiseaux has invited me here for a reason, she reminded herself.

She squared her shoulders firmly. "I'm a seamstress," she whispered again, this time with a little more confidence. She squeezed her paws together.

Someone cleared their throat, and Delphine glanced up with a start. The guard had lifted her visor. "You may enter now," she announced. Then she gazed at Delphine more gently. "The princess is very kind," she said. "You have nothing to fear."

And at that, the double doors swung inward.

Chapter 4

an exquisite antechamber stretched before Delphine, filled with more beautiful objects than she had ever seen. Velvet sofas, damask curtains, candle-lamps, petite chaises, a harpsichord, a sparkling vase overflowing with white flowers. Delphine struggled to take it all in. The entire opposite wall was made of windows that overlooked the castle's formal garden. From up here, it looked like a grand forest of hedges.

A young pawmaid gestured through a doorway. "This way, mademoiselle."

Delphine approached. Through the doorway lay another room, even larger and more elegant than the first. And in the center, admiring herself in a full-length looking glass made of a jewel-encrusted human hand mirror, stood Princess Petits-Oiseaux. A huge pet bumblebee hovered lazily alongside her on a spiderweb leash.

At the sight of Delphine, the princess squeaked with joy. "Oh! The seamstress!" Princess Petits-Oiseaux handed the bumblebee's leash to a nearby pawmaid. "Ysabeau, be a dear and take Bearnois to his perch." Then she sashayed across the room with delicate steps, despite her massive skirts. "You're here! How delightful! And right on time!" Her wig swayed, minuscule figures of angels dangling precariously from the curls. She laughed gaily. "You shall make me the most fantastic gown!"

Before Delphine could think of how to respond, or how to express her gratitude at being invited to the castle, Princess Petits-Oiseaux continued unabated. "You know, I am quite tired of these old things." She gestured languorously at a heap of gowns lying over a nearby sofa. "Nothing new. Nothing fresh. Nothing . . . *fantastique!*" The princess laughed again, sounding like the tinkling of a bell. Her perfectly waxed whiskers arched gently, and Delphine noticed the curlicue whisker right away.

The princess, Delphine could see, had a fashion style all her own. Her long neck was set off by a high collar at the back of her bodice, while the front dipped sharply into a frothy ruffle of gold lace. Her panniers jutted out from either side of her waist, making her skirts so wide that Delphine doubted she could have touched either side with paws outstretched. A quirky mixture of sparkling jewels fought for the place of honor around her neck.

"Forget about all of this," the princess commanded, waving at her own garments. "I summoned you because I saw your fantastically unusual gown on Lady Roselle Beaux-Neiges. I should love for you to sew an even more fantastic gown for me." The princess sank onto a sofa like a flower delicately landing on water. Her pawmaids bustled around her, arranging her skirts and bringing her a clear, round globe. Delphine watched in fascination as the princess tipped it to her lips, drinking delicately.

"Rose water," the princess explained. Then she gestured at one of the pawmaids. "Ysabeau, darling, bring our guest a goblet of her own."

Ysabeau traipsed brightly across the rug to where a massive rose petal was sitting on a wide table, half-filled with water. She dipped another globe into the water, then presented it to Delphine, who realized it was a human bead, cunningly sealed at one end. The water tasted exactly how Cinderella's roses smelled when they first opened. Heavenly.

"Now." The princess patted her paw imperiously on the sofa,

barely able to reach over her right pannier to do so. "Let me tell you about this ball. Whenever the human royals choose to throw a party, we do as well. And why not? They provide the music, the food, the entertainment . . . All we have to do is head to the ballroom we've constructed inside their chandelier, and enjoy."

Delphine perched on the sofa next to the princess, trying desperately to look as if any of this made sense to her. She nodded vigorously.

"The next ball is to be at dusk in one week's time—alongside the human prince's ball. I wish to wear something fantastical, something unlike anything that has been seen before."

Delphine's mind was racing. A ball at dusk . . . the stillness of twilight, and the arrival of evening. The sky coming to rest as the stars begin to show themselves.

The *stars* . . .

Delphine let out a little squeak of excitement, then clapped her paw over her mouth, mortified. Her manners!

But the princess leaned forward eagerly across the sofa. "Yes? Yes, my darling? Do tell!"

Delphine's eyes sparkled. She could feel the fizzy delight of a wonderful idea already rushing through her blood. "A gown that transforms you into . . . the First Star of the Evening Sky," she said raptly.

Princess Petits-Oiseaux fell back on the sofa with a look of shock on her face, eyes squeezed shut. Her pawmaids all gasped in unison and pulled out tiny fans, ready to spring into action if the princess were to faint.

What did I say? The bottom dropped out of Delphine's stomach.

Then the princess's eyes snapped open, and she sat bolt upright. "I *love* it!" she squealed, clasping her paws together. "It's *merveilleuse*! It's brilliant! It's new!"

The pawmaids all sighed in relief, tucking their fans back into their own small panniers.

"Oh, I'm so glad, Your Royal Highness!" cried Delphine.

The princess leaned forward with curiosity. "How do you imagine it will look?"

Delphine began to describe her vision, slowly at first, then with growing confidence. The princess nodded enthusiastically as Delphine spoke.

When she had finished, Princess Petits-Oiseaux clapped her paws together. "Perfection!" She sprang up from the sofa. "I shall await your return, with the gown."

Delphine's heart sang. She couldn't wait to get back to her workshop and begin on the design.

"Stop by our fabric storerooms! Take whatever you need!" said the princess. "They have my measurements as well! Farewell, my sweet seamstress." And just like that, the meeting with the princess was over. She hadn't even needed her measuring tape!

Delphine was in heaven as she waltzed out of the princess's

chambers. She was so much in her own world, in fact, that she didn't even see Alexander stepping in front of her for another deep bow before it was too late. She ran straight into him with a squeak of surprise.

"Oh!" Delphine blushed right up to the tips of her ears. Her very first visit to the castle, and she had already managed to knock over one of the lords, albeit a pompous one.

He pulled himself upright, shaking out his cloak and grinning at her. It looked like a genuinely amused smile for a moment, and she felt a little less embarrassed, but it was so quickly replaced by a carefully composed suaveness that she almost doubted she had seen it. "My lady." He made another deep bow. "I have awaited you so that I may have the pleasure of escorting you back to the main hall, or to wherever you are next headed."

Delphine stifled a sigh, but said as sweetly as she could, "I'm going to the storerooms. The fabric and trim storerooms." She gritted her teeth thinking of how many more tales of his derring-do she would have to endure as he escorted her.

Alexander's eyes were suddenly bright. "Are you a seamstress?"

"Uh . . . yes?"

He started swiftly down the hall. "Come, my lady!" he entreated with an honest enthusiasm she'd not heard from him before. "I must show you a great secret of the castle! I've never shown a soul, but *you* . . . you should see this!"

Delphine's curiosity was piqued, despite herself. She knew she should be gathering supplies. But she couldn't resist the temptation of a secret.

She followed Alexander through the corridors until they reached the open archway that she had seen before. It was just as dark and foreboding on the other side.

"Through here," said Alexander nonchalantly.

Delphine hesitated. "But I thought you said that was the Forbidden Wing."

"We'll be fine." He slipped each of the guards a few gold pieces and quickly escorted Delphine through.

On the other side of the archway, her eyes adjusted quickly to the dim light. She could see a long, narrow bridge extending across a pitch-black crevasse. She had no idea how deep it was, and she didn't want to find out. The bridge itself looked incredibly rickety, as if it had been purposely made of the thinnest wooden scraps that the architects could find. She could barely see the far end of the bridge, it stretched so far into the darkness.

Suddenly, a flicker of light caught her eye. Alexander stepped out blithely onto the bridge, carrying one of the torches that had been resting in wall sconces next to the guards. He beckoned for her to follow.

"Is this bridge safe?" Delphine couldn't help but ask, stepping onto it with great trepidation. The narrow strips of wood felt like they were buckling beneath her.

"Oh yes," he said in a jaunty tone, striding forward into the dark. "It's perfectly safe for mice. It was constructed that way intentionally, after the wing was abandoned." His voice echoed back and forth between the crevasse walls, and he stopped talking abruptly.

When they finally reached the other side of the bridge, Delphine found herself in a human-size hallway, though it was clear no one had lived there for centuries. Dust lay thick on every surface. The fashions in the giant paintings were hundreds of years old. The air itself felt heavy with silence, broken only by the odd ominous rustle. "I thought you said this was part of the mouse castle," she whispered to Alexander.

"This part was walled off by the humans long, long ago. We're just passing through it now on the way to our real destination. After the War to End All Wars, drawing the boundary at this hallway seemed like the natural solution. The rats had always spent more time over here than the mice, it's said, so they were banished to this side and the mice were assured safety once again."

Delphine stopped dead in her tracks. "Rats?"

He turned to glance back at her. "Oh yes, the rats. That's why it's called the Forbidden Wing. And that's why the bridge was built with such delicacy—it can bear the weight of mice, but not of rats. Very clever, those engineers of yore."

Delphine was standing extremely still. "So there are rats in here?"

"Certainly." He shrugged coolly. "But the treaty takes care of that. They don't bother us, and we don't bother them. Besides, if the rats don't see us, we'll be perfectly safe." He saw the look on her face. "I myself roam here from time to time. It's a bit of a lark among the nobles, really. We dare one another to scamper through the Forbidden Wing, usually reciting poetry as loudly as possible."

It sounded like the sort of silly hijinks that she and her friends had engaged in when they were much younger. But she bit her tongue.

"And . . . *why* exactly are we safe?" she asked instead.

"Because of this." He pulled back his cloak and revealed a sword resting in a sheath at his side. The sheath was made of richly tooled leather with the crest of the castle on the main panel, and precious gems were inset along the pommel of the sword. "I always have my trusty blade at hand."

Delphine was not convinced. It had been drilled into her since birth that rats were some of the most dangerous creatures in the kingdom.

Alexander noticed the look on her face, and softened. "Ah, well, the rats *are* a threat, of course," he admitted. "But I know all the side paths and shortcuts. We'll be fine."

Delphine eyed him. She wasn't convinced he could take on a rat, yet she also wanted to know more about the promised secret. She gestured down the hall. "Please lead the way," she said, gathering her skirts with one paw in case they needed to make a dash for it. But the hallway remained silent and motionless, with no sign of rats, and eventually they passed through a wide hole gnawed in the wall.

She thought of the treaty Alexander had mentioned. As a young mouse she had been taught about the Great Betrayal of a century ago, when all the rats of the kingdom had turned evil without warning, slaughtering as many mice as they could before the mice had rallied and fought back. She knew of the War to End All Wars, and how all the other creatures—voles, shrews, frogs, and salamanders—had stood alongside the mice to stop the rats' carnage. It had been an uneasy truce, these last hundred years, but it was all she and everyone in the kingdom had ever known. It was strange to think they were exploring chambers that hadn't been inhabited for so long.

Alexander led her along narrow ramparts and down steep staircases, deeper and deeper into the darkness. "We're going down into the tunnels beneath the castle. Nowadays it's the only way to reach the hidden rooms." He faced her. "You've heard the stories of the Threaded?"

Delphine laughed. "They were only my favorite tales when I was little! Along with Sir Guardefois and the Seven-Headed Cat . . . oh, and Princess Elsabet and the Magical Milk Pitcher."

But Alexander wasn't smiling. He was staring intensely at her, eyes gleaming. "The Threaded were *here*."

"Here? Where? Peltinore?" Delphine blinked. "What are you talking about?"

"In this very castle! I found proof!" He gestured widely, then sighed. "But nobody believes me." His elegant whiskers drooped a little, and Delphine almost felt sorry for him.

They turned down another dark, narrow corridor. Despite the faint, flickering light of Alexander's torch, she saw only blackness at the other end. A cold breeze rolled slowly around their ankles, oozing out of the darkness ahead. The air smelled like mildew, like root plants rotting in a storeroom—the smell of slow decay.

After a few more minutes, Alexander led her over a narrow stick balanced across a waterway, and they began to head upward again, climbing steeply. Delphine breathed the fresher air with relief. Finally, they reached a pile of abandoned barrels. Alexander wriggled behind them, gesturing for her to follow.

On the other side of the barrels was an old human comb leaned sideways against a wall. "I dragged this in here," said Alexander proudly. "So that I could get through that opening." He pointed upward to a crumbling hole in the wall.

She followed him up the comb, climbing the teeth like rungs on a ladder, through the hole. She found herself standing in a long, mouse-size hall. A series of open alcoves had once provided places where lords and ladymice could sit and chat. The alcoves were all still decorated in luxurious furnishings of the previous century, but the dust was so thick it looked like fur had sprouted on every surface. The silence was complete. It was as if she had stepped back in time.

Alexander grinned at the look on her face. "This is part of

the wing that was abandoned by the mice when the treaty was enacted. It's been here ever since, closed away and forgotten.

"I stumbled across the entrance years ago," he continued, threading his way down the hall on tiptoe.

Delphine wondered why he was walking so delicately until she stirred up a little eddy of dust and was immediately seized by a sneezing fit.

"I spent hours examining the frescoes, the delicacy of the brushstrokes." He stopped in front of an alcove with what looked like filigree etched into the walls. Even under the mask of age, the gold still gleamed faintly. "Then I reached this one."

Delphine took a step forward. "It's lovely," she murmured.

The back wall was decorated with a frieze of Arachne the Mortal and Rhapso the Nymph. Delphine remembered learning about them from tales of classical mousethology, archived in the books of the mouse library in the château. The two figures stood facing each other, whiskers nearly touching, a thin golden thread suspended between their paws, upon which a small spindle hung. Overhead stretched an archway of gold roses. Their tails intertwined with the stems. She took another step closer.

"Look," Alexander said, almost whispering as he traced his pawtips along the archway of roses.

Now that he was pointing it out, she could see a hairline crack all along the edge of the archway and down either side to the floor. "It's a *door*," she breathed.

"Correct." He reached out and pressed on the spindle in the frieze. It must have triggered a hidden mechanism, because the entire panel started to slide away. Daylight peeked around the edges of the panel as it moved backward. Then it ground to a halt, daylight spilling through the narrow opening.

"That's as far as it seems to open," Alexander said. "The contraption must be ancient. It's a miracle it still works. But we can squeeze through. I've done it before."

Something was pulling at Delphine, some impulse deep within her. Alexander's words about the Threaded being real . . . She needed no encouragement to head inside. She pressed herself against the opening, squeezing her head through, whiskers brushing against the walls, then the rest of her, careful not to snag the lace of her apron against the rough stone walls.

On the other side, the narrow entranceway widened into a perfectly round room. She realized she was inside one of the decorative sconce towers that hung on the outside of the human castle's spires. Windows ran nearly floor to ceiling along the opposite side of the room, but she didn't even notice the view—what she noticed were the *tapestries*.

With colors still glowing softly after so many years, beautifully sewn hangings lined the walls, bringing to life scene after scene of the Threaded—mice sewing flower petals together, embroidering runes onto snail saddles, stitching incredible and elaborate garments that sparkled like glittering stars.

Then Delphine saw what they were holding. She gasped.

The world seemed to stop as she stared at the long silver needles that the mice in the tapestries were using. She thought about her mother's tale of her Finding: how the air had always shimmered in one special spot on the little doorstep. How one day, the shimmer was gone and a baby had appeared in its place. How that baby had come with nothing except a strange needle. Tarnished, blackened, looking like a piece of scrap metal, and unlike any needle the Desjardins mice had ever seen. As large as a human needle. Delphine's only legacy.

Now Delphine gazed at a dozen massive silver needles, clutched in the paws of the twelve magical Threaded mice of lore—*just like hers*. Their needles were gleaming, new, but they were unmistakably the same as the one that hung on her wall.

Delphine felt the blood rush out of her head, and dizziness overtook her just as Alexander entered the room behind her. He ran to her side, barely managing to catch her as she fell. Tingles ricocheted through her body at his touch, and she struggled to sit up.

"I'm all right," she managed to squeak. She couldn't stop staring at the tapestries.

Alexander followed her gaze. "I told you the Threaded were real," he said. "This proves it, doesn't—?"

She turned her eyes to his, her gaze burning. "Alexander." The words tumbled out of her, unthinking. "I—I have one of those needles."

Interlude

R ien ran down the hallways, not knowing where he was going, just that
he had to get away. Tears streamed from his eyes and he blinked them
back angrily. If only he could find a place to hide, just for a few hours, until
the other servants forgot about taunting him and went back to their jobs. He
hadn't asked to be the littlest rat in the kitchens, just like he hadn't asked to
be the runt of his litter.

The stone hallways that crisscrossed under the vast fortress were nearly always empty. He kept running, turning this way and that, until he was certain he had lost his pursuers. Then he let himself slow to a walk. He rubbed his face with a dirty sleeve, whiskers damp with tears.

He hated them. No, he didn't hate them. He refused to hate them. It wasn't their fault that they were so cruel, all those he worked with in the kitchens. He saw how they were bullied in turn by those above them. If he were ever in charge someday, he would be kind to everyone, no matter who they were or where they had come from.

Rien turned a corner and ran right into a young mouse who had been coming from the opposite direction, her snout in a book. They both jumped in surprise at seeing someone else there, and the book fell from her grasp.

"Sorry!" He grabbed it off the floor and pushed it back into her paws. Then he noticed how she was dressed. She was clearly one of the mice from upstairs. He blushed so deeply that his ears turned red. He had never been permitted to speak to one of the upstairs mice before. He was nothing more than a lowly, twig-thin rat in threadbare clothes, still just a child, barely old enough to be put to work.

She took the book from him. "Thank you." He realized she could only have been a few years older than he was. "I would have been in trouble if it got damaged," she said. "I wasn't supposed to borrow it, you see."

"Why are you down here?" he asked, suddenly wary. Had one of the kitchen staff sent her to drag him back for punishment?

"I have a habit of sneaking down here when all of my lessons and practice become too much," she said. She spoke softly but clearly, enunciating *every syllable. It was music to his ears, unlike the coarse tones in the kitchen.*

He looked back down at her paws. "What is that?"

She turned it so that he could see the painted birch-bark spine. "The Tale of Arachne and Rhapso. I'd rather read this than study, you see."

"Oh."

"Have you read it?"

He looked down. "Read? Well, I . . . no . . . I don't, I mean, I can't . . ."

Understanding dawned in her eyes. "Oh! Would you like me to show you how?" she asked.

He hesitated, unsure if this was a trick. "I'm not supposed to talk to you," he said finally.

She glanced up and down the empty hallway. "Nobody needs to know."

He looked at her, unsure how to respond.

She smiled. "I don't want to go back upstairs anyway. Come on."

He followed the mouse to a little archway he hadn't even noticed before. Inside was a long, padded bench, hidden from view, next to a narrow window that let in the daylight. She seated herself on the bench and gestured for him to join her.

At first, she showed him the words in the book, turning the onion-skin pages one by one to point out the various letters and how they were used together. But soon they were joking and laughing, the book forgotten.

The mouse sighed happily. "I wish every day could be like this one. I'd rather stay down here with you. They're all so boring up there. Sometimes my lessons are fun, but I wish I could just have a friend to play games with. I never get to play any games."

"We could be friends," Rien blurted. He immediately shrank back, horror spreading across his face. How could he have proposed such a thing to an upstairs mouse?

But she smiled back, her eyes luminous and lovely. "I'd like that."

the camembert m●●n

Chapter 5

all the way back to the chateau, Delphine could think of nothing but the needle hanging above her bed. Her heart was in her throat as the cart jostled over byways and around winding bends until it finally came to a stop in front of Château Desjardins. Then she climbed down and hurried inside, fabrics from the castle storeroom piled high in her arms. What was her old needle doing in tapestries that had been created—and then abandoned—so many years ago? Was it a clue about where she had come from? She didn't see how that could be the case, and yet the coincidence was too impossible to ignore.

Rushing inside, she dropped all the fabric on the parlor table in an untidy heap. She had to see her needle right away. As soon as she was in her cozy, crooked bedroom, she snatched it down from the wall. Yes, it seemed similar to the ones in the tapestries, with those strange, swirling symbols carved into its surface just like the others. She ran her paw along the cold length of the needle as she had done so many times before.

I could head back to the castle right now, she thought. *Compare it to the tapestries. Just to be sure.* She even bent to slip her shoes back on, but then stopped herself. Maman would want to know she'd returned safely. And, of course, there was the little matter of having just one week to create the finest gown she'd ever made.

With a sigh, Delphine carefully placed the needle back on its hooks in the wall. She could take it with her when she returned to the castle to deliver the dress. Somehow she would manage to wait.

✳ ✳ ✳

Delphine quickly found that her daily duties plus the added task of the princess's gown left little time to dwell on the needle and tapestries.

Every morning, she sat on her stool in the château sewing line, stitching away on sensible garments for the residents, while in her mind's eye she planned out the intricate details she would embroider onto the princess's gown.

"Head in the clouds again, Delphine?" the older mice asked good-naturedly. They were used to her fancies. And Delphine merely smiled back at them.

Then there were the rest of her chores. During the Monday sweeping of mouse hallways, corridors, and stoops, she used the time to do the math in her head for the number of tail's-lengths of lace she would need around each layer of the petticoats. On Tuesday afternoon, when everyone helped wrangle the ladybugs as the garden was being strung with new netting, she stood lost in thought, mesh stretched across both paws, picturing how to create just the right flounces. Nursery duty, on the other hand, took every ounce of her attention and energy to put the pinkie mice to bed.

After dinner each night, her mother kissed her on the forehead between the ears. "Let me know if you need anything," she'd say, and then Delphine would hasten down the corridors toward her workshop. Finding she wasn't satisfied with just the materials from the castle, Delphine dug through all the scraps of fabrics she'd been hoarding since she first started watching Cinderella make garments. Some of the silver-colored pieces were especially perfect, and Delphine laid those aside.

For hours upon hours, she sewed by the light of the candle ends. In the parlor below, Cinderella labored over her stepsisters' gowns, as well as her own, for the human ball. Whenever

Delphine felt she couldn't sew another stitch, she would look down at Cinderella sewing away industriously, and find the strength to go on.

After a while, it seemed as if Delphine had flounced more flounces than had ever existed in the history of gowns, embroidered more buttonholes than could possibly fit onto a single garment. Still, she kept on as each day dwindled like the wick on a candle end.

Maman stopped by in the evenings with a tray of piping-hot caraway-seed cookies or freshly roasted parsnip slices. She would implore Delphine to take a break and have a bite to eat, which she would do for a few moments. But then Delphine returned to the task at hand, sewing and sewing away.

✳ ✳ ✳

Thursday dawned clear and sunny—the perfect laundry day. Work paused as all the mice of the château took the opportunity to do their washing. Delphine and her mother hung up their damp, now-clean garments on the clothesline they had stretched across one of Cinderella's window ledges. Far in the distance, the castle stood proud on its hilltop, gleaming in the morning sun. Delphine set each split-twig clothespin carefully as she went, her mind getting a chance to return to the needle.

"Maman," she finally began. She had spoken to her mother hundreds of times about the story of her Finding. But somehow, this time it seemed different. More urgent. She took a deep breath. "You remember when you found me?"

Her mother chuckled. "The happiest moment of my life."

"You always say that," Delphine replied with a little smile. "But didn't you ever wonder who left me there?"

Her mother looked solemnly at her over the clothesline. "Of course."

"Do you think it was my birth mother and father?" said Delphine in a small voice. One of the many, many questions that had plagued her ever since she could remember.

"There's no way to know," replied Maman. "But whoever it was, I'm sure they loved you, and it broke their hearts to leave you behind."

Delphine turned away, gazing out over the rolling French countryside. The castle was a sparkling cut-crystal vase, the turrets and flags looking for all the world like bunches of flowers leaping over the vase's edge. The sun glittered off the river as it curved its way through the fields and pastures. The world seemed so beautiful, so at peace. Delphine wished she could feel the same. The restlessness she had always felt was now growing in leaps and bounds. It was as if the tapestries of the Threaded had sparked a flame inside her.

She struggled to find the words. "I just wish I *knew*, once and for all." She stopped, fearing she sounded unappreciative of everything that her mother had done for her.

But Maman stepped close to her, wiping her paws on her

apron and then placing her arms around Delphine. She cradled their heads together as she had done when Delphine was very young. "I understand," she said. "Chérie, I've always known you would want these answers."

A little breeze came around the corner of the tower and fluttered the clothes on the line, pulling at a petticoat. It threatened to spring free of its twig clothespins.

Delphine ran to repin it more thoroughly. "How would I even know where to begin?"

"Well," said her mother, rejoining Delphine, "you just need one place to start. When you unravel a line of stitching, what do you do?"

Delphine paused. "Pull out the stitches one by one?"

"But first?" her mother prodded.

"Find the knot." Delphine saw exactly what Maman meant. "You find the knot! You cut it!"

"Exactly. And then what happens?"

"One after another, the stitches all come undone," said Delphine slowly. In her mind's eye, she saw the needle hanging over her bed, waiting to be taken to the castle.

She would find the knot.

✳   ✳   ✳

All too soon, Friday arrived. It was the last night before the ball. Maman volunteered to take Delphine's shift in the nursery so that she could get a few extra sewing hours. Delphine was all too happy to accept.

She hurried through the passageway to her workshop, heading past the stepsisters' bedrooms. Even through the wall, she could hear them both screaming at Cinderella to start over on their dresses. Delphine gritted her teeth in sympathy. *Poor Cinderella.* She scurried on, up a tiny spiral staircase and past the grain storage barrels that the kitchen mice had slowly been filling for winter.

Inside Delphine's workshop, half-finished pieces of the princess's gown were strewn across every surface, all in various states of embroidery, beading, trimming, stitching, and finishing. Delphine sighed. Like Cinderella, she had her work cut out for her. But it was still early, and she had plenty of time to finish, if she just focused.

At that moment, the pitter-patter of little claws on wood sounded in the hallway. A head popped around the doorway, full-cheeked and wide-eyed. "Delfeenie! At your service."

"Gus!" Delphine cried, a grin spreading across her face. She hopped off her spool-stool and flew across the workshop, hugging her friend so tightly that the bright green cap fell off his head. "What are you doing here?"

"Come to help, of course!" She could see that he was carrying a paper packet of marzipan tarts under his arm. "Whatever you need, Delfeenie, just say the word." He placed the packet on one of the spool-stools. "I even brought snacks, hot from the oven."

Delphine was touched by his kindness. Marzipan tarts were a rare treat.

A rumbling suddenly filled the hall, and then Jaq appeared, rolling several candle ends through the doorway. He bustled around the room to determine their optimal placement, and in no time, Delphine's workshop was better lit than it had ever been.

Thus passed the rest of the night, with the three friends working to finish every stitch, bow, and embellishment on the finest ball gown to have ever been created at Château Desjardins.

But with every stitch of her tiny mouse needle, Delphine thought again and again of the human needles she had seen in the tapestries. It was strange—a week ago, an invitation to the castle was the biggest thing that had ever happened to her. Now her world seemed to be expanding even further, unfurling before her like a giant patchwork quilt.

Delphine wondered . . . what answers would tomorrow bring?

Chapter 6

Delphine rifled through her drawers, scrambling to find a clean outfit to wear to the castle. How could she have not planned this the night before? Rays of morning light were already streaming through her window. She upended acorn-cap containers full of tail-ribbons, then dug through the folded laundry on top of her dresser to find an apron. At the last moment, she snatched up her traveling cloak against the early-morning chill that was becoming more and more prominent as fall began to take hold.

The princess's gown was just where Delphine had left it, hanging in the middle of her workshop, wrapped carefully in an old sheet. All of the accoutrements sat alongside it in a big drawstring sack. She unhooked the wrapped bundle from the beam and managed to wrangle it through the passageways to the mouse front door. Outside, a few early risers greeted her merrily, including Cittine and Margeaux.

"Back to the castle, Delphine?" chirped Cittine.

"Is that the dress, then?" trilled Margeaux.

"Yes, and yes!" called Delphine.

"We'll help you when the cart arrives!" they twittered.

Delphine positioned herself alongside the turnaround where the carts always stopped. Today, it would be the cheesemonger. There was still dew on the grassy stalks nearby, and she kept the dress bundle well away. She could keep the drawstring sack off the ground by slinging it across her back. Then came the clack of the horse's hooves on the stone pathway to the château as the anticipated cart drew into sight.

Delphine stayed back until the cart had come to a stop and the human had descended, whistling with her delivery of fresh cheeses. As she headed toward the servants' door of the château, Delphine scampered toward the cart with her bundle in tow. It took a lot of pushing by Delphine's paws and lifting by Cittine's and Margeaux's beaks, but they finally managed to get the precious dress loaded into the back of the cart. She climbed in alongside it, waving adieu to Margeaux and Cittine as they fluttered back up to the tower ledge.

Then Delphine shot upright.

The needle!

It was still hanging over her bed.

Without a moment's hesitation, she ran to the side of the cart. No cheesemonger. Hopefully she was still inside, enjoying a morning croissant. Hurriedly, Delphine dove over the side of the cart and ran back to the château, sack still slung over her shoulder.

Heart racing so fast she thought it would burst, Delphine threw open the mouse door and dashed madly through the passageways. Her mother had already left, probably to head to the kitchen for the fresh crumbs Cinderella always saved for the mice of the château. *Just as well*, Delphine thought. She wouldn't have wanted to explain why the needle was suddenly more important than the gown. Truth be told, she wasn't certain herself.

Dashing into her bedroom, Delphine yanked the needle off its iron hooks. Then she impulsively grabbed the old linens that had been draped alongside it, and wrapped them around the needle as protection. She managed to wedge it into the bag holding the extra baubles and accoutrements for the princess, like a quiver holding a very long arrow.

Delphine rushed out, slamming the door behind her and

praying that she hadn't made any of their glasses fall off the shelves in the process. She bolted back down through the passageways and around the twisting corners. She could barely breathe. If the cart left without her . . . with the dress inside . . .

Scrambling through the front door, Delphine saw the cart still waiting. Relief coursed through her. She scurried across the gravel path, nearly to the cart.

And then Lucifer emerged from around the corner of the château garden. His tail lashed from side to side, green eyes flashing. His lips curled in a sly smile, flashing sharp teeth. Before she had a chance to react, he was already running pell-mell across the dirt toward her, his eyes frenzied with a look that gave Delphine chills.

She broke into a mad dash, the sack with the baubles and needle banging against her back. She reached the bottom of the cart. Her first desperate leap got her close to the wheel spokes, but not close enough. She could feel Lucifer's hot, foul breath on the backs of her ears. She leapt again, managing to dig her mouse claws into the wood of the spokes. Lucifer swiped his paw and she barely dodged it, then scampered up the side of the cart as the paw came back again in the other direction. Scrambling onto the top edge of the cart, she dropped the sack inside and leapt down after it, out of pouncing distance and harm's way.

Delphine collapsed in a heap, feeling the rough wood under her fur. All she wanted now was to make it to the castle without anything else going wrong. She could hear Lucifer hissing angrily from the ground, clearly too well-fed to leap up onto the cart himself.

Human boots crunched on the gravelly stones, and then the cart gave a huge shake as the cheesemonger hoisted herself back up onto her perch and clicked her tongue at the horse. The cart pulled forward, settling into a gentle rhythm along the country road. Delphine peered over the edge of the cart to see Lucifer prowling before the château in the distance, growing smaller by the second.

The other animal passengers spent most of the trip dozing. Delphine wished she could do the same, but adrenaline was still coursing through her, and her nerves were raw with tension. At least changing carts at the crossroads didn't seem as intimidating this time around, and a friendly passenger helped her transfer the gown. The arrival hall in the castle courtyard was as wild as before, but now Delphine was prepared. She got the bundle down from the cart with the assistance of a court lackey and entered the massive entrance hallway. Now she just had to find a valet to help her. She squared her shoulders and began to look around.

A familiar face appeared in her vision. "Lady Delphine! What a charming surprise!"

Oh no.

Delphine took a deep breath. She was determined to behave like a court mouse, even if that meant putting up with Alexander. How would a noble respond politely? "Y-yes!" she stammered.

"I mean, likewise! I have returned with the gown for the princess." She gestured to the massive bundle.

He bowed low. This time, he was wearing a plum velvet waistcoat and vest with silver brocade lining the slashed sleeves. He held a matching velvet cap in his paw. "What a lucky turn of events that I should be here at this moment."

"Yes." Delphine wasn't fooled. He knew perfectly well that she would be back today with the dress, what with the royal ball being that night. She gave him a quick, hard stare, but he smiled back pleasantly, eyes innocent.

"Will you allow me the pleasure of escorting you to the princess's quarters again?" he asked.

"I would, uh, be delighted." That sounded pretty courtly of her, didn't it? "But how will we carry the gown? It's rather heavy."

"Milady, I shall procure a catercart."

"A *cat* cart?" she squeaked, but he was already gone.

She glanced around, still awed by the grandeur of this massive hall. This time she noticed a few mice here and there dressed in a more simple style, similar to hers. That made her feel better. At least she wasn't the only common mouse visiting the castle that day. *Or perhaps they work here*, she thought.

Alexander returned with a wooden cart pulled by two furry caterpillars. A leaf hung in front of the caterpillars for steering purposes. Alexander deftly navigated the catercart into place, loaded the gown into it with care, then gestured at the sack and her travel cloak. "Would it please you to place those in here as well?"

She swung the sack from her shoulder, and he positioned it onto the cart.

As he did, the eye of the needle poked out of the top of the sack. Alexander's mouth opened and he glanced at Delphine, then back at the needle. For once, he seemed to be at a loss for words.

"I brought it," she said, not sure what else to say.

"Then—" He swallowed. "Then it's real?" He reached out a paw and touched the cold metal. "Incredible. A needle of the Threaded."

"It might be, but . . ." Delphine hesitated. "I need to go back to the tapestries to compare them."

"Of course!" He ran his paw over the few markings that weren't hidden. "Could these be letters of some kind?" he mused.

"I've wondered that, too," she admitted. "But it's impossible to make them out clearly. The needle is so tarnished. I've tried polishing it more times than I can remember. I think those markings are just lost to time."

"Fascinating." Alexander tucked the needle back into the bag, rewrapping it snugly. "Shall we head now to the princess's quarters, my lady? Afterward, I would be honored to escort you to the tapestries once again!"

"I would love that," she said, realizing that she had been so focused on getting the needle to the castle, she hadn't even thought about how she would find her way back to that closed-off room. Maybe it was a good thing that he had been waiting for her after all.

Alexander led her along a path of wide ramp-ways clearly made for animals with wheeled conveyances. She marveled at the cleverness of the catercart as Alexander guided the caterpillars with a flick of the leaf at each turn. And almost before she realized it, they had reached the princess's quarters.

✳ ✳ ✳

Dressed in the new gown, Princess Petits-Oiseaux stood in front of her mirrors, gazing at Delphine's work. The panniers lay like two evening clouds atop mounds and mounds of pale nighttime silk, draped to form the main skirts. *All the beading was worth it,* Delphine thought, watching how the sunlight glittered on the starry details of the bodice. Under the full moon, it would twinkle in just the same way.

The mouse princess clasped her paws together in delight, squeaking, "It's absolutely perfect!" She gazed over her shoulder into another mirror, admiring how Delphine had interwoven strands of silver thread to create a cobweb of gossamer over the skirts and up the center of the back. The tiniest seed pearls fluttered delicately all around the hem of the skirt, thanks to the hours of hard work the night before.

One of the princess's dainty hind paws emerged, clad in a matching night-silk slipper. "You've thought of simply everything!" she gushed. A crystalline crown sat nestled between the princess's ears, creating a halo of sparkles all around her. She truly was the First Star of the Evening Sky.

The pawmaids scurried around her, fluffing the gossamer on the skirts and fiddling with the draping of the panels. Delphine stood back, her work finally done, happy to take it all in.

The princess clasped Delphine's paw and pulled her up onto the pedestal beside her. "Thank you, my little seamstress," she said softly. "My fairy seamstress. You are truly magical."

Delphine looked at the two of them in the mirror. Next to the princess and her perfectly curled whiskers, she was just another commoner. But in that moment, she felt as radiant as the princess looked.

"You must make another gown for me!" Princess Petits-Oiseaux exclaimed. "We always have so many balls. The Autumnal Ball, the Winterberry Ball, the Valentine Ball . . ."

Delphine's mouth dropped, but she regained her composure and hopped down from the pedestal so that she had enough space to curtsey. "It would be my pleasure," she said, stealing one of Alexander's favorite lines.

"Wonderful! Now don't forget to stop by the kitchens before

you go. The food they're preparing for the festivities is simply marvelous! They'll give you a little taste." Then with a clap of her paws, the princess was lost in a sea of servants crowding about her.

Her work done, Delphine exited the royal chamber, eager to head to the hidden tapestries. But the hall was empty. It seemed her guide had disappeared. She chewed on her lip in frustration. Being beholden to *Alexander*, of all mice . . .

Delphine wandered through the hallways, inquiring of every half-friendly guard she came across, but nobody had seen Lord Alexander Perrault. She flagged down catercart drivers, even inquired of the mice who operated the dumbwaiters that lifted heavy wares from floor to floor. Alexander was nowhere to be found. And Delphine was getting grumpy, not to mention hungry.

Well, the princess *had* encouraged her to sample that evening's wares. Making her way to the kitchens, Delphine tasted every dish—twice. She was about to go back for thirds when she suddenly noticed that the sun was setting. She had no desire to venture into the Forbidden Wing in the dark.

Shoving her way through the crowds of servers, Delphine exited the kitchens and moved into the crowded hallway. It seemed as if the entire castle were there, headed for the ball. This was hopeless. But just when she was on the verge of giving up, she spied a familiar face on the other side of the hall, and he looked positively flustered.

Alexander!

Delphine raised her paw to wave, and his face lit up. "Lady Delphine!" he called, doffing his cap from across the hallway. He struggled to cut through a cavalcade of flagon-loaded carts passing between them, each flagon filled to the brim with dandelion mead and secured on the cart with a few twists of spiderweb. Upon reaching her, he went for a deep bow and swept his cloak directly into the face of a sweaty hedgehog page, sending him flying.

Horrified, Delphine rushed to pick the little hedgehog up off the floor and help him gather his wits. She gave him her handkerchief—he looked like he could use one—and sent him on his way. She could hear Alexander behind her, beginning his regular series of introductory pleasantries.

"Such a joy to finally espy you here, in this unexpected locale, when I have been searching all throughout . . ."

She cut him off, a bit more curtly than she meant to do. "Are we going to the tapestries now?"

"Well." He paused, and she realized that he had changed outfits since she had last seen him. He was now decked out in a cobalt velvet surcoat and gold-embroidered waistcoat. "I had been planning . . ." He coughed, a bit awkwardly.

"You were planning to go to the ball," she finished.

"Yes, but with you! Or at least, that had been my hope. . . ." He bowed low once more. "Would you do me the privilege of allowing me to escort you to—"

Delphine put out a paw, kindly but firmly. "I would love nothing more than for you to escort me, yes . . . but to the tapestries. Please."

He hesitated only for a moment, and then his debonair persona returned. "Then let us return to the tapestries, as promised."

✳ ✳ ✳

The empty hallways of the Forbidden Wing echoed with every step Delphine and Alexander took. Delphine's head whirled, wondering just what it would mean if her needle truly was one of the mystical Threaded's. Then ominous shadows loomed up in front of them, dispelling all of her musings.

Delphine's heart stopped.

Rats.

Alexander pulled her into a dark recess in the wall. "Hush!" he whispered. They listened to the eerie clicking of claws on stones fading into the distance.

Breathing a sigh of relief, the two mice continued to the hidden entrance of the room where the tapestries hung. Alexander again pressed on the golden skein, and the panel opened just enough for them to squeeze through. Night had long since fallen, and the moon was hidden behind a thick wall of clouds. But Delphine had stopped caring about being in this part of the castle at night. She had a mystery to unravel.

Delphine tiptoed from one tapestry to the next, studying the twelve mysterious mice who made up the Threaded. She drew out the needle from her bag and compared it to the ones held by the mice of legend. She could see instantly that it was the same size, same shape of the eye, similar runes on the shafts.

Her ears trembled in disbelief, but it was undeniable. She held a needle of the Threaded in her paws.

She looked at Alexander. "If it were polished and gleaming . . . it would be identical."

Alexander nodded. He had been standing silently beside her. Now he leaned over and rubbed a paw on the dull surface, but the tarnish remained, ancient and stubborn, like storm clouds frozen in time on the once-silver surface.

Delphine moved to the tapestry closest to the window, hoping to catch some starlight in the dark room. Just then, the clouds parted. A thin moonbeam shone down directly onto the needle in her paws. In an instant, the metal went from ice-cold to positively hot in her grasp.

"What—" She nearly dropped it. "It burned me!"

Alexander reached out curiously, then pulled his paw back, staring at her with an odd expression. "My lady . . . it's freezing."

The clouds drew back still farther, and as more of the light from the full moon spilled down onto the needle, it almost seemed to *tingle* in her paws. Was that the right word? Just the slightest sensation, but she could feel it if she concentrated.

The last wisp of clouds vanished from the face of the moon,

and its light poured into the room, washing over the needle. As it did, the tarnish began to fade, like breath disappearing from a mirror. The engravings were becoming more and more visible. But just as suddenly as it had started, the magic stopped, leaving only a small patch of the needle glowing bright and silver. The rest was as dull and cloudy as it had always been.

Shocked, Delphine gazed down at the needle. It lay quiet in her paws, with one small silver area now gleaming in the full moonlight. The few symbols that had been revealed looked more like animals than letters, curled in on themselves. They were masterfully engraved into the surface of the needle, almost as if the silver had simply melted and re-formed into those shapes. But the metal felt cold once more.

Something was tingling again, a strange, fizzy feeling inside her head.

She looked up to see Alexander staring at her, slack-jawed.

"Your whiskers," he barely breathed.

Then Delphine realized there was a shimmer in the corners of her vision, little prickles of light.

Her whiskers, her strange gray whiskers, were turning to silver, starting at the tips and radiating inward like arcs of light being drawn in the air.

In a moment, they were shining as brightly as the silvery patch of metal under her paw.

IN A DARK ROOM STOOD a dark throne, a twisted, broken throne, cobbled together from bits and pieces of scrap over long years of waiting. On the throne sat a rat, biding his time. He stared into emptiness, his face covered in scars. Ears notched, snout askew, eyes burning black with hatred. A rat so huge that he could have fought a fox and won. He had waited this long. He could wait a bit longer.

His guards patrolled the fortress. Prisoners wept in their cells far below. Time ceased to have any meaning. He would wait until he could wait no more.

Then the clouds outside rolled back from the face of the full moon. In that instant, a burst of pain shot through him, searing his scars. He leapt up in agony, eyes rolling in his head, lips pulled back in a horrible grimace.

In another instant, the pain was gone, leaving him with only one thought:

It has been found.

Chapter 7

" Then this truly was a needle of the Threaded," Delphine said to Alexander as they headed back through the grime and stench of the lower tunnels. "But how did it make its way to me? Did whoever left it with me at the château even know what it truly was?"

They crossed up from the tunnels back into the abandoned wing, heading down the human hallway. Their paws trod silently on the moldering carpet of centuries past as Delphine carried on.

"The answers have to be out there somewhere. Alexander, this is really happening! I finally have a *clue* to where I came from! Don't you see? I can't believe this!" Her voice echoed in the cavernous human hallway.

Alexander laughed nervously, looking around. The massive drapes on either side of the cracked oil paintings hung motionless. "It's wonderful, my lady, it is, but please, let us speak quietly until we reach safe ground."

She nodded distractedly. "Of course."

The bridge out of the abandoned wing was just ahead. They tiptoed another few paces, but Delphine just couldn't help herself.

"And my whiskers!" she whispered loudly. "How did that happen? I've had gray whiskers since I was a pinkie mouse, Maman tells me so. This needle must truly have powers! Could that be? Could such things be real?"

Alexander shot out a paw in front of Delphine in warning, but it was too late. The drapes ahead began to twitch. With a terrible hiss, one rat and then another and another came surging out from behind the fabric. The two mice spun around to see even more rats coming toward them from behind.

"Run!" screamed Alexander. Delphine nearly tumbled over her own paws, but managed to scramble forward, still clutching the needle tightly. It glittered in the dim light as they ran.

She could feel the hot, rank breath of the rats on her tail. She sprinted faster, gasping, and then threw herself through the entrance to the old bridge.

It had been designed to only hold a mouse's weight, Alexander had assured her, but it suddenly seemed far too sturdy as they rushed across. The guards on the far side, used to having the most uneventful post in the castle, looked up astonished as the two mice ran toward them at full speed.

"Rats!" Alexander squeaked as they reached the guards.

Delphine could now hear the rats snarling on the other side of the bridge, but Alexander had stopped running entirely.

"They'll never come over here," Alexander panted. "It's all in the treaty."

But the bridge was starting to sway. Fangs dripping, the rats had begun to climb across. The fragile structure buckled under their weight, but still they pressed on.

"Invasion!" cried one of the guards. He smashed his armored fist against the bell hanging alongside the archway. The old metal clattered, shaking off the hundred years of dust and cobwebs that clung to it.

The other guard had taken hold of his halberd, shifting his weight nervously from paw to paw. A third guard entered through the archway from the castle proper, slamming down the visor on her helmet. She gave a guttural roar and charged out onto the ledge, pointing her halberd directly at the oncoming rats.

The rats snarled and froze, but Delphine could see more skittering along the underside of the bridge, climbing upside down, horrible grins spreading across their faces.

"It's not supposed to bear their weight!" cried Alexander. "They're going to make it across!"

One particularly vile-looking rat was perched on the top of the bridge, a dirty cap hanging askew from one ear. He turned and screeched at the rest of his troops. "Get that needle!"

The words hung in the air, and the mouse guards redoubled their grips on their weapons.

The needle? Delphine thought wildly. *Why do they want my needle?*

"Get that needle!" the rat cried out again. "And kill that filthy mouse who holds it!"

Delphine's blood ran cold as the rat leapt into the air, propelling himself toward the far ledge with such force that he landed on top of several incoming mouse guards. He rose back up, kicking them to either side, spittle flying from his jowls as he snarled. "Onward!"

The bridge began splintering as more rats threw themselves onto it. Several had already reached the near side and were crawling up over the ledge.

Delphine screamed and fled into the now-crowded hallway, Alexander racing behind her. It seemed the sound of the old alarm bell had thrown the castle into an uproar, mice squeaking madly to one another.

"They've crossed the bridge!"

"They've broken the treaty!"

Delphine and Alexander suddenly heard a horrible crash behind them, followed by terrified howls.

"The bridge!" cried Alexander. "It's finally fallen!" He glanced over his shoulder and froze.

Delphine looked back to see that a group of rats had shoved past the guard mice. They were climbing over the other mice, but they weren't fighting. Nor were they attacking any of the other castle residents, who were running madly in every direction.

They were heading straight for Delphine.

She turned and sprinted full-tilt, knowing even as she did that it was no use. On open ground, rats could run faster than mice. Of all the things she had been taught over the years in avoiding the perils of rats, that was always the number one thing to remember. Outmaneuver them. Outclimb them. But *never* try to outrun them.

Delphine spotted the dumbwaiters ahead. It was risky, but anything was better than being torn to pieces by rats. She leapt into the nearest one, Alexander following behind her.

"This is a bad idea!" he shouted, but Delphine had already unhooked the pacing rope.

In the next instant, the bottom dropped out from under them with a sickening shock as the dumbwaiter fell like a stone. The wind blew fiercely in their whiskers, floor after floor of the castle speeding past them. Then the bottom of the shaft came into view. Stones flew up at them, and they landed with a thump.

Delphine squeaked loudly and rolled out of the basket, heading toward the nearest door. Alexander rushed behind her, fumbling with his scabbard. "Delphine! What's so special about that needle? They haven't broken the treaty and crossed the bridge in a hundred years!"

From above came the clatter of claws on stone. The rats were climbing down the shaft's walls, straight toward her.

"I have no idea!" Delphine reached the door and seized the latch, yanking it open. She found herself back in the huge hall where she had first arrived.

A sudden deep booming sound shook the entire hall around them. The castle's clock tower was beginning to strike midnight.

She broke into a run, heading toward the exit to the courtyard. She was a mere tail's-length away when a sleek-furred rat leapt in front of her with a snarl. She froze, heart thumping wildly. She had never been this close to a rat before.

Turning, Delphine ran back into the sea of mice. She dashed through an archway to find a little side door, its hinges nearly rusted shut. Delphine slammed her shoulder against the wood, Alexander doing the same beside her, until the rust groaned and the door swung open into the stable courtyard.

A forest of horses' legs, stamping and tromping, stretched out before them. Coaches rolled past as human coachmen with their massive boots clomped back and forth. Out here, the striking of the clock tower was even louder.

Alexander scanned the courtyard. "We can get back inside over there."

Delphine looked to where Alexander pointed, seeing nothing but the stone walls, massive barrels, and horses with their terrifying hooves.

Then a high keening sound cut through all the roar of the courtyard.

Delphine spun around, her blood running cold.

The first of the rats had emerged through the door. It peeled back its lips and made the same high keening cry again, like the wail of a banshee.

It was calling its companions.

Delphine scampered up the side of a pile of house-size crates, claws digging furiously into the wood, Alexander climbing alongside her. Another sonorous boom came from the clock tower. She cast about desperately for anything that could help them. Then she noticed a curious sight.

A silvery coach, round like a pumpkin and sparkling in the moonlight, had just pulled away from the front steps of the castle and was heading toward the gates. Maybe, just maybe, if they timed their leap perfectly . . .

She scrambled to the top of the crates, jammed the needle through several layers of her skirt fabric, and turned to find that Alexander had fallen behind. The bloodthirsty creatures were gaining on him. Delphine panicked. As much of a fop as he was, she wouldn't leave anyone to the rats.

Suddenly, Delphine remembered the rats' curious behavior in the hallway, shoving past the guards, ignoring the other mice. They were focused solely on her.

And the needle.

Perhaps she could save herself *and* Alexander at the same time.

The silver coach approached, its horses so close she could smell their warm, sweet breath as they clip-clopped by. She had only one chance. She didn't dare look down, didn't dare think of what would happen if she missed. As the coach drew alongside the crates, she gathered all her strength and leapt.

She flailed madly, reaching out with all four paws. Her tail thrashed as she smashed into the side of the coach and slid downward, but she managed to grab on to the gilded paneling of the door.

"Delphine!" came a frantic cry.

She gazed back to see Alexander at the top of the crate stack, staring at her in horror.

Yet her gamble had paid off. The rats were turning in midstream, no longer heading toward Alexander and the pile, but across the courtyard toward the speeding coach.

"Wait! Stop!" New voices entered the scene as dozens of humans spilled down the front steps of the castle. Human guards on horseback suddenly appeared from around the corner in pursuit of the coach. She watched in horror as the rats leapt at them, clawing their way up the horses' flanks as they whinnied in pain. Now the rats were riding the horses.

The coach passed through the castle gates just as the clock struck yet again. As they careened down the road, Delphine gripped the paneling with all her strength. The coach raced on, dashing across the bridge and over cobblestones. But when Delphine glanced back, the human guards on horseback were still just behind . . . and that meant so were the rats.

There came a cry over the howl of the wind. She looked down at the coach runners below.

"Delphine!"

It was Alexander, hanging on to one of the filigreed loops that sprouted up from the carriage wheels. "Just hold on!"

"*I am!*" she yelled back, but her words were swallowed up in the din.

Another hairpin turn, and the coach went up onto two wheels. Delphine screamed and buried her snout in her cloak. The coach crashed back down onto all four wheels and sped onward.

A distant bell toll came floating faintly through the cold night air. It was the last stroke of midnight. The door panel beneath Delphine's paws gave a sudden wriggle, like a dog shaking off a flea. She startled but managed to keep her grip. Then there was another tremor, even more pronounced. She stared at the silver trim—was it fading away before her eyes? The panel shuddered once more and then vanished entirely, leaving nothing but the smooth side of the coach, now a strange silvery orange. She shrieked, falling backward, thrashing madly. She heard

Alexander call out in surprise as she landed with a thud in a pile of dandelions. A moment later, she heard another thud nearby.

What happened to the coach? Delphine's head was spinning, but she knew the only thing that mattered now was getting out of sight. She pushed herself up just in time to see the coach disappear around another bend in the road, decorative spirals coming loose and flapping wildly as it went.

Hearing the other horses' hooves thundering up the road, Delphine ducked back down behind the dandelions, watching them ride past. Many had rats still clinging to their saddles. She shuddered.

When she was certain that the last horse had passed, Delphine carefully made her way toward where she had heard the other thump. Sure enough, there was Alexander, heading in her direction. She sighed in relief. Anything would be better than being stranded out here on her own in the middle of the night.

But before she could ask him if he was all right, he swept into an elaborate bow. "I'm here to save you," Alexander announced with a flourish of his cloak. "I bravely leapt onto the coach so that I could take you back to safety. I knew you would need me."

Ugh. His pomposity was too much to bear.

She turned away from him, scanning what lay beyond the road. Nothing but dark forest, as far as the eye could see. An owl hooted in the distance.

Alexander now reappeared in her view. "My lady . . . may I assist you?"

"I'm going to go find a safe place to wait for morning," she huffed, stalking away.

"Good plan, my lady!"

Hearing him running to catch up, she sighed and continued deeper into the forest, away from the road. The horses would be heading back to the castle at some point, and she didn't want to be there when they went past with their rat stowaways.

Delphine chose a safe-looking pile of leaves and burrowed in deep until she was completely hidden and relatively warm. She had no idea what sorts of predators might be lurking in addition to the owl she had heard, but she didn't want to take any chances. Then she peered out of her makeshift nest to see Alexander standing in front of it, paw on his sword.

Delphine stared at him. After a few minutes, his chin drooped slowly but he continued to stand doggedly upright.

"Why don't you get some sleep, too?" she asked finally.

Alexander shook his head. "I shall stand guard all night, my lady," he replied, still gazing out across the moonlit forest.

She sighed. "Whatever you wish." Wrapping her cloak tighter around her, she closed her eyes. The leaves she had burrowed into were dry and sweet smelling. She felt the needle resting beside her, solid and reassuring. With a shuddering breath, Delphine fell asleep.

She awoke late that night. Poking her head out of the leaves again, she spotted Alexander fast asleep on the ground under a piece of bark, drooling into his fur. *Ha.*

Moonlight beamed down, and the needle caught her eye, lying alongside her in the leaves. The silvery bit of the inscription shimmered, and Delphine gazed at it. The words seemed just out of reach, so close that she could nearly hear them. She reached out to clutch the needle and fell back asleep with it resting in her grasp.

Commandant Robeaux slipped down from the exhausted horse onto the cobblestones of the castle courtyard, and cursed under his breath. He turned back to the rest of his legion, all in various states of disarray.

"How could you let that needle disappear?" he roared.

The rats managed to look everywhere except at him.

He growled in irritation. After years of castle duty—a pointless assignment given that the mice controlled the entire grounds—he had finally stumbled upon the key to advancing his station. Only for it to slip through his paws like mincemeat.

One sullen rat piped up. "What's the big deal with a needle, anyway?"

Commandant Robeaux turned the full power of his gaze on the whiner, who had the decency to cower under his look. "Haven't you ever heard of King Midnight's obsession with needles? He has a whole wall of them in his throne room."

"Never even met King Midnight," the rat muttered, and a few of the others nodded.

The commandant scoffed. "Well, I have, and I've seen his wall of needles. Eleven of them, all as large as human needles, covered in markings just like that one. And let me tell you, he's been saying for years that if anyone were to ever find another, it'd be worth its weight in gold. *More* than gold. And he'd make the rat who delivered it the new leader of his army." He crossed his arms, but there were still glazed expressions on the faces of most of his squad members.

"There are needles everywhere," said another rat, picking her teeth with a claw. "Just steal another one."

"Not like that one, there aren't," spat back Commandant Robeaux.

It was useless, trying to convince this lot of the importance of the needle. He pointed to the cleverest of his rats. "Victorine. Figure out where that coach was going. We're finding that needle, even if it means killing that nasty little mouse. The rest of you, hurry up and get back to our side of the castle before we bring the whole treaty down around our ears. And don't lay a paw on a single one of those castle mice!"

But as Robeaux gazed into the distance, he wondered if they should shift tactics. *Treaty be blasted.* He was going to get that needle to King Midnight, at any cost. Nobody would prevent him from finding glory this time.

the bleu moon

Chapter 8

The next morning, Delphine looked and felt exactly as if she had fallen off a moving coach the night before. Alexander, on the other hand, somehow appeared as fresh and dapper as a mouse who had slept in a comfy bed instead of on the hard dirt. She gritted her teeth in irritation as she tried to pick bits of dry leaves off her skirts. It was useless.

"Refreshed?" he asked cheerily, and she fought the urge to smack him.

"I'm just happy to be here," she replied in a forced bright tone. She tightened her travel cloak around her and started walking, needle in one paw. Alexander fell into step next to her.

She looked at him. "Are you following me?"

"Simply ensuring your safety. And curious about your destination?"

Delphine considered as she walked. "Not back home, not until I know that the rats won't follow me there. If they knew where I lived . . ." The thought was too awful to bear.

Alexander coughed politely. "My lady, perhaps the best course of action would be to return to the castle. May I escort you?" He was walking at a painstakingly slow pace.

"The rats are there," Delphine said as she marched on.

Alexander caught up to her. "True, but . . . do you by chance have an alternative destination in mind?"

"Of course I don't." She turned to face him. "But I have to do something! I have nothing, no clues, no idea where to go. All I have is—"

"The needle?" he supplied.

She nodded, tight-lipped.

"And you're certain that it can't help point you in the right—"

She groaned. "Yes. I've been staring at it since before I can remember. There's nothing there." But she unwrapped it from the linens anyway, holding it out to him.

He studied it carefully, then sighed in defeat. "Hmm . . . yes, indeed. I don't see any clues, either." He took the linens from her paw, rewrapping the needle carefully. "Why do you have Tymbale linens, anyway? That brotherhood has been gone for years."

Delphine stared at him. "*What?*"

"The linens." He pointed at the embroidered design. "That's the crest of Tymbale Monastery. When I was little, I studied the old crests of all the houses and clans and brotherhoods and sisterhoods and knighthoods. It's incredible how many there are, but you can get really good at recognizing them if you take the time."

Delphine was tearing the linens off the needle, spreading them out to get a better look. "You *know* what this crest is?!"

He looked at her a little oddly. "It's Tymbale. I— Didn't I just say that?"

"Yes, but . . ." She grabbed him. "I've asked every guest who's ever come to the château to look at it, and nobody has ever recognized it."

He shrugged. "I guess I had a lot of free time as a child."

Must have been nice, thought Delphine, remembering the countless hours she had spent on chores and housework before and after school.

"This is . . ." She paused to gather her thoughts. "This is a real clue. You said 'Tymbale Monastery'? Then I'm connected to that monastery somehow. Maybe I came from there. Maybe my birth parents lived there!" Her face lit up. "Where is it?"

"Where *is* it?" Alexander gave a glib laugh. "I have no idea where it *is*. That sort of information isn't important when memorizing old crests. Symbolism is important. The design, the colors, the shapes, that sort of thing."

Delphine fought the urge to scream. "So then," she said very slowly and deliberately, "what *can* you tell me about Tymbale?"

"Well . . ." He took the linens again and gazed down at the crest. "If I recall correctly, it was founded by badger monks, who designed the crest centuries ago. These three shapes here that look like unicorn horns represent courage . . . but they're green, which stands for loyalty. Then this orange thing . . . maybe it's a crest of feathers? That means ambition, but also . . . obedience." He looked up at her, confused. "That doesn't make much sense, does it?"

She snatched them out of his paws. "No, it doesn't, Alexander. Because those aren't unicorn horns. Those are cypress trees. They're *green* because they're *trees*."

"Trees?"

"I've been staring at this crest over my bed every day of my life. I'm pretty certain."

He pointed at the orange plume of feathers. "Then what's this?"

"A fox. Obviously."

He scrutinized it. "A fox . . . Wait a minute. Delphine! I know what this is referencing!"

She cocked her head at him.

"Fox Rock. East of here. It looks exactly like a fox. I remember it from my cartography studies. And—oh!" He jumped in excitement as something else occurred to him. "It's right next to a cypress forest!"

"Great." She wrapped up the needle once more. "Then we go to Fox Rock, and I'll figure it out from there. Lead the way."

Alexander wrinkled his nose. "This has been admittedly enlightening, but I really must insist that we return to the castle, for your safety—"

She turned, no idea which way she was headed other than it was away from Alexander. "I'm going to go find Fox Rock. You can come with me or not." She started walking. A moment later, she heard Alexander coming up behind her.

"My place is with you, my lady. I leapt onto that coach to protect you, and I shall continue to do so." She could practically hear him puffing up his chest as he spoke.

∗ ∗ ∗

Hunger was fast setting in. Delphine had been watching for wild nut trees or berry bushes for hours with no luck. Then, through the thick branches in front of them, came a strange sight. Something huge and orange was peeking through the undergrowth.

Alexander peered over her shoulder. They could make out the shape better as they grew closer: giant, smooth, resting on massive green leaves, vines twisting neatly up from the dirt.

"A pumpkin!" breathed Delphine.

She couldn't guess how it had been missed by all the hungry forest dwellers, but there it was, large and plump enough that Delphine and Alexander could have hollowed it out and lived inside.

Her mouth watered as she thought of all of her favorite pumpkin dishes—tarts, soup, éclairs, nutmeats, sausages, butter crêpes. . . .

Alexander came up beside her. "What is this thing?" He drew out his sword, ready to poke at it.

"Wait!" Delphine reached for his arm. "Don't just go filling it full of holes. There's a right way to do this, and it's certainly not by starting down here at the bottom."

He grumbled at Delphine's instruction, but removed his cloak and sword belt, placing them alongside the pumpkin as Delphine did the same with her own cloak and the needle. Then she gestured for him to follow as she climbed up on top.

"You start here"—she pointed to one side of the stem—"and I'll start there, and we'll gnaw all the way around in a circle."

The look on Alexander's face was spectacular. *"Gnaw?"* he said disbelievingly. "You mean with my *mouth*? On that thing?"

"It's a pumpkin, and yes. Haven't you ever eaten pumpkin?"

"Well, yes, but . . ." He twisted his cap in his paws. "I didn't know that it came from something that looked like this."

"I'll show you what to do," she continued. "It won't hurt you,

I promise. Watch." She demonstrated how to neatly nip through the surface of the pumpkin. "And then you just keep going. Look, I can do the whole thing on my own if you like, but—"

Her gambit worked. "No, no! I wouldn't dream of it." He jammed his cap back on his head a little more firmly than necessary. "I'm ready."

Working in tandem, they moved around the stem. Then, with a few stern kicks, the whole round top fell inside with a wet thud.

Alexander jumped. "It's empty?!"

Delphine was realizing just how sheltered he had been growing up in the castle. "Yes, Alexander," she replied. "Pumpkins are basically hollow inside." She crawled down into the interior. "But not *entirely!*" she called, gathering an armload of the slimy pumpkin pulp and dragging it back up toward the entrance. "Take this!" She shoved the glop up through the hole.

"*Beetles and boils!*" came Alexander's voice. "You expect me to touch that?"

She sighed. Why had she even asked? "I'll do it." Worming her way around the edge, she hauled the glob of pulp onto the top and let it slide over and down to the ground.

Alexander looked slightly ill.

"Well, one of us will be having a delicious dinner. The other one can just watch." She fished out a few more armfuls, then dragged the pulp to the edge of the clearing and piled together some dry twigs into a little fire. Alexander hovered, fascinated.

"You've never seen anyone build a fire before, have you?" she finally said.

He shook his head, still watching. "I thought you lived in a château."

"A château that is in the countryside . . . and we have picnics and bonfires all the time. Don't you?"

He shrugged gracefully. "Of course. Catered by the royal kitchens, staffed by the royal servants, with live music and marble furniture to create that certain ambience."

"*Marble* furniture? For a picnic?" It was Delphine's turn to shake her head in disbelief.

The pumpkin seeds sizzled and spat in the fire. When they were brown and crispy, she flipped them out with the quick poke of a green twig she had broken off a nearby bush. The shells were so hot that the mice burned their paws on them, but they were too hungry to care. They gobbled them down, picking out the morsels of sweet nutmeat.

"Those were delicious," Alexander said drowsily, his head pillowed against a log.

Delphine rolled her eyes. "Not so bad after all?"

"Not so bad." He yawned.

Thin afternoon sun trickled down into the little clearing in the middle of the forest. Delphine sighed. Her belly full and her fur warm, she felt her eyes grow heavy.

✳ ✳ ✳

Even before she had awoken completely, Delphine knew something was wrong. She held perfectly still, cracking open one eye just enough to survey the scene. There was Alexander, snoring away. The fire, burned down low but embers still glowing. The pumpkin, nestled in its vines. Then a movement caught her eye, just behind it. A rank odor hit her nose, and she knew instantly.

Fox.

"Alexander," she whispered as quietly as she possibly could.

He snored on.

"Alexander."

Terrified to move, but more terrified to remain where she was, Delphine felt around until her paw met a pebble. She tossed it in Alexander's general direction, not taking her eyes off the pumpkin.

She heard it thud softly against something, probably his leg. He snuffled. "Quiet!" she hissed. "Listen carefully. There is a fox, just behind the pumpkin. If it hasn't spotted us already, it will any moment. The only hope we have is to fight."

She dared a glance over in Alexander's direction. He was wide-awake by now. He slid his paw down his side. "My sword!"

"I know. The needle, too. We put them over there, remember?" She nodded toward the little pile of leaves to the left of the pumpkin. "We just need to get to them."

"You want to run *toward* the fox?" He would have been screeching if he hadn't been keeping his voice to a whisper.

"What other choice do we have? We can't outrun a fox. But we *can* fool it. I have a plan."

Alexander listened as she talked, nodding slowly. "Not a bad idea. It's still absurd, of course." He gathered himself. "But I'm ready when you are."

She waited for a moment, listening, then squeaked, "Go!"

They sped toward the leaf pile as fast as their paws would carry them. The closer they drew, the stronger the fox's odor became. Delphine could feel it filling up her nostrils like the smell of mildew and death. She scrabbled for the needle and could hear Alexander grabbing up his sword.

Then a dark, wet nose nearly as large as Delphine's head came around the pumpkin, drawing in a deep sniff of air. They froze. Long white fangs appeared as its lips curved back in a deadly smile, its pitch-black eyes shining with evil.

"Climb!" Delphine screamed. The mice leapt at the pumpkin, grabbing tight to the surface with their claws. They scrambled to the top and dove down inside. The fox pounced, fangs crashing together where they had been standing moments earlier. It snarled in rage.

Delphine and Alexander slithered underneath the stem piece that they had pushed inward, now lying at the bottom of the pumpkin. It was cold and wet, but it was also thick and sturdy. It would make an excellent shield against the claws of a fox.

The pumpkin rocked to and fro as the fox struggled to shove its snout into the opening, but the hole was far too small. It snarled again, refusing to give up. Delphine prayed it wasn't smart enough to figure out how to roll the pumpkin over, though even if it did, she believed their claws could grip deep into pumpkin meat for a very long time.

Luckily, they didn't have to test that theory. The fox's snout withdrew, replaced a moment later by a paw. The fox swiped from side to side, clawing in every direction. But Delphine was ready.

Needle and sword drawn, the two mice knelt behind the pumpkin lid, watching as the sweeping paw drew closer and closer. "Wait for it," whispered Delphine. "One, two, three!"

Just as the paw passed above their heads, they stabbed forward in a concerted effort. The fox yelped in surprise, then clawed more furiously than before.

"Begone, vile creature!" squeaked Alexander. He stepped out from behind the lid, then slipped on the slimy interior and fell flat on his face in some of the remaining stringy pulp. Delphine watched in horror as he struggled to get free but instead became even more intertwined with the pulpy strands. The paw flashed downward once more.

Delphine leapt forward, needle outstretched, jabbing like wildfire at the fox's paw, until it finally withdrew with another yelp. A moment later, they could hear the thumps of the fox's footfalls as it retreated into the forest.

She turned to the pumpkin-covered lump that was Alexander. "Would you like some help extricating yourself?"

He wiped a large glob of pulp from his surcoat, ears pink with embarrassment. "That would be lovely."

✳ ✳ ✳

They slept underneath a pile of geranium leaves and found themselves soaked by the dew in the morning. *Not the best start,* Delphine thought. But at least they were on their way to the monastery. "We'll catch the next vehicle headed east," she said as they breakfasted on leftover pumpkin seeds.

Alexander shook his head. "Too dangerous. The rats know we traveled here by coach. They'll assume we'll continue to do so, and check every coach within a thousand paw's-lengths. We should keep walking."

Delphine stared at Alexander. That was the last thing she had expected him to suggest, and it sounded like a recipe for disaster. She couldn't imagine he'd ever walked farther than the castle gardens in his life. "Are you sure?"

Alexander straightened to his full height. "I shall withstand any travails to protect you, my lady."

Let him find out just how hard it is to travel like a common mouse, Delphine thought. "Very well," she said. "Let's go, then."

Delphine doggedly set the pace. It was a long day, and by the time the sun was touching the horizon, she was ready to lie down right there in the grass. But she knew better. Alexander, blissfully ignorant of the dangers, had rallied to keep going "and make use of the moonlight" until Delphine pointed out an early owl coasting overhead. After that, Alexander was even more enthusiastic than she was about finding a safe place to hide for the night.

Day after day, step after step, they traveled, hiding in the undergrowth whenever a coach passed. The roads were dusty when dry, and slippery when soaked by rains. They spent their time alternating between choking on dust and squelching through mud.

Delphine quickly realized that she needed a new way to carry the needle, ensuring that it was both out of her way and reachable. Most importantly, it needed to be completely hidden.

When they happened upon an abandoned human glove by the side of the road, she spent an hour gnawing off long pieces. That evening, she wove the leather strips into a proper sheath by their twigfire as Alexander watched, intrigued.

"Voila!" She slipped the needle inside, then slung the strap across her chest.

"Wonderful," Alexander remarked. "Reminds me of the time I was midbattle with some pesky ants and had to cobble together a sheath for my extra sword."

As they walked, Alexander continued to regale her with tales of his derring-do, interspersed with anecdotes of court life. To Delphine, each story seemed more outlandish than the last. It was painfully obvious how little he'd actually experienced of the world outside the castle walls.

Life on the road was tiring. Luckily, the early-autumn nights were still warm. Nourishment was another story. Delphine was used to gathering snacks from bushes and trees when she, Gus, and Jaq had gone on afternoon picnics, but she'd never had to sustain herself solely on what she found.

As for Alexander, if it didn't come on a silver platter or in a cut-crystal bowl, he wouldn't have known it was even edible. Delphine did her best to teach him about plants as they went, in the hopes that he could help scout for food, but Alexander seemed singularly incapable of identifying anything.

After this happened for the umpteenth time, Delphine had had enough. "How is it that you can tell whether the lilies on Lord Beetle-whatever's surcoat were embroidered with silk thread or cotton thread, but you can't tell the difference between burdock leaves and dandelion leaves?"

Alexander bristled. "I told you that story in confidence."

Delphine let out a deep sigh.

While they hadn't seen hide nor hair of a single rat on their travels—*yet*—rain proved a constant threat. If they didn't scramble onto the nearest rock or branch quickly enough, they could be washed back down the road.

Delphine kept reassuring herself that soon they would reach the monastery and she would find the answers she needed. But each night stretched into the next. And there was no sign of the elusive Fox Rock that Alexander remembered so clearly from his studies.

Then one morning brought a dawn bright and chilly. Delphine and Alexander were crossing a field, their fur dampened by the frosty dew. Delphine had been keeping an eye out for any fresh herbs or berries that could make up their breakfast when they were suddenly rewarded by the sight of an eerie pile of rocks up ahead, dark against the sky. Lichen clung in scattered bits to the surfaces of the stone. The air felt oddly quiet.

"I think that's it!" Alexander breathed as they approached.

"Fox Rock?" whispered Delphine. There didn't seem to be any immediate danger, but there was something about the place that made her fur stand on end.

Alexander nodded. "It's the wrong angle, though. In all the illustrations I've seen, it looks like a fox. Let's get closer."

With another few steps, Delphine's perspective shifted. The stones lined up so that she could make out a long, narrow out-cropping shaped exactly like the snout of a fox. Two empty holes formed dark eye sockets. Long shards of pale stone hung down, looking like cruel fangs waiting to strike. Delphine shivered, reminded of the fox they had evaded at the pumpkin not so long ago. The wind suddenly rattled through the trees around the rock, then fell silent once more.

"No wonder it's called Fox Rock," she muttered.

Alexander pointed upward. "And from this angle, it looks exactly like the fox in the crest!"

She saw what he meant. Following the stone fox's gaze due north, she noticed cypress trees in the distance.

"Let's get going," Delphine said, picking her way through the dead grass around the base of the rock and heading toward the far trees.

They left the clearing, but not before Delphine had glanced over her shoulder one last time. Fox Rock stood silent, its empty eyes gazing menacingly at them. She shuddered again, wondering when she would finally be able to return home.

KING MIDNIGHT PACED IN HIS throne room. His tail lashed, nearly upsetting a side table and spilling the flagon of bloodred berry cordial that rested on it. How many years had he been staring at his wall of needles? The thought was like a thorn in his paw.

He passed the wall yet again, glancing up out of habit at the eleven needles hanging there. Silent. Dormant. It was pointless. He had tried everything to unlock their mysteries, prise out their magic. And not one glimmer. Not one spark.

But then, when he had least expected it, that horrible pain. He barely dared to hope. Could it mean the final needle had been found at last?

He rubbed at the silvery scars that crisscrossed his body, the one across his face like a forked bolt of lightning in an angry storm. "This idiotic, endless war," he growled, slamming his fist onto the table. The flagon of cordial jumped. That absurd treaty the mice had backed them into accepting. Let them think that they had found peace. He could bide his time until he finally had enough power to eliminate them all.

Timid knocking came at the doors.

"Enter!" he roared.

A rat in a tattered uniform tiptoed in, flanked by King Midnight's guards.

Midnight eyed him angrily. "How dare you disrupt my contemplation!"

"You'll want to hear what he has to say, m'lord," ventured one of the guards. "He's a messenger from the Forbidden Wing of the castle."

That explained the ragged uniform with the red braid. Midnight couldn't remember the last time he'd had a messenger from the castle rats, and with good reason. They had little to do but keep their wing occupied, waiting until the treaty could be broken and the rats finally seized power.

The messenger coughed nervously. "Commandant Robeaux sent me, King Midnight."

Midnight picked up the flagon to pour himself a glass of cordial. "Go on."

"He's sighted another needle, your Midnight-ship, sir," said the rat, trembling now.

The flagon slipped from King Midnight's paw, crashing and spilling onto the wood floor. So it was true. He hunched over and gripped the table, staring at his razor-sharp claws but seeing visions of victory.

"I know it sounds crazy," the rat babbled, "but I swear I saw it, too. I was there when—"

"Enough!" King Midnight thundered. He turned on the castle rat. "You say you saw this needle?" He spoke softly, slowly, like a snake hypnotizing its prey.

The messenger twisted his paws together. "Y-yes, my king. Carried by a little gray mouse in the company of a noblemouse."

King Midnight's voice dropped to a whisper. "And this little gray mouse . . . you let her get away?"

The messenger gulped. "Not on purpose—"

"Castle filth!" King Midnight roared. He dashed at the messenger rat, fangs bared. With a single swipe of his massive head, the messenger was no more.

He turned back to his guard, breathing heavily. Blood dripped from his mouth. "Clean that up," he ordered, gesturing where the messenger lay.

Then he turned back to face the wall of needles.

A thought began to revive itself from long ago, when he had still held out hope of finding the last one. Perhaps they all needed to be brought together to work. That would explain why he'd never been able to get any of the other needles to perform even the slightest spark of magic.

"Summon Snurleau!" he roared. He would send his very best spy to confirm the needle's existence.

King Midnight's tail twitched as he imagined row after row of magicked rat troops storming the castle and taking over the kingdom. His silver web of scars writhed as he shrieked with laughter. Then he wiped the tears from his whiskers, still chortling with wicked glee, and tossed his cloak back over his shoulder.

He had a needle to find.

Chapter 9

A gray wall of clouds hung low in the late-afternoon sky, making it nearly impossible to see anything from the cypress branch where Delphine was perched.

She could hear Alexander calling up from below. She ignored him and clambered a few branches higher to get a better angle, trying to peer ahead. Still nothing. If only the autumn fog would lift.

Then her eyes caught a ghostly shape looming through the gray. *A tower?* It had to be. She squeaked in excitement. It was so close! They could be there in half a day. Delphine scampered back down the trunk to rejoin Alexander.

"Did you see the monastery?"

"Yes!" Delphine felt hope rush over her. "At least, I think so. There's a tower just ahead. What else could it be?" She grabbed the makeshift sheath that held the needle. "Let's go!"

The cloud wall hung so low that it permeated the air with its damp. They strode forward, Delphine keeping an eye on what little she could see of the sun to ensure they were heading in the right direction. "Let's hope we find answers."

"Or at least a safe place to spend the night."

"Afraid of sleeping in the woods again?" She ducked under a low-hanging branch.

Alexander cleared his throat. "Of course not. This is nothing in comparison to the dangers of the hawkworm invasion a few years back." And he was off again with his tales of heroism in the face of inescapable odds.

As they walked, Delphine stared through the trees, deep in thought. The needle had come from the Tymbale Monastery and looked exactly like those of the Threaded. So perhaps this place had been their headquarters. That would make sense, given that it was now abandoned. But none of that explained how or why the needle had ended up with her. She sucked on a whisker absentmindedly. Where had the needle been for the last hundred years, before it was stitched through her baby linens?

Just as dusk gave in to the falling night, the massive fir trees parted before them. Crumbling stone walls rose up out of long-forsaken gardens. A tower sat high atop the main building, all carved plinths and ivy-covered escarpments. Flying buttresses that had once reached for the sky now lay crumbling in various states of decay. Some of the outbuildings had lost their roofing and stood as no more than four empty walls. But a few appeared to still be in habitable condition, more than one would expect from a place long abandoned. And through the stained-glass windows of the main building, light was flickering.

"There's someone inside!" squeaked Delphine, nervously wrapping her tail around her ankles.

They tiptoed across the forlorn gardens as quietly as they could, keeping an eye on their surroundings. The massive wooden doors stood silent and barred, looming up in front of them. Since the monastery had been built by badgers, the doors seemed huge to the mice. They stared at the ancient wood, studded with iron nailheads and scarred by years of wind and snow. *Behind these doors lie answers*, Delphine thought.

"I'm going in first," whispered Alexander. He placed his paw firmly on the door handles.

"You are *not*," argued Delphine, stepping in front of him. "It's my quest."

"I'm here to protect you, remember?" He tried fruitlessly to wedge himself between her and the doors. "It's the chivalrous thing to do."

"Oh, nutmegs to you and your chivalry. It's not your needle, and you're not the one the rats want to kill."

"Precisely why it's all the more imperative that I go in first!" Alexander fumbled for his sword.

Delphine took the opportunity to place herself even more squarely in front of the door handles. Now that she could see them clearly, she realized that there was neither lock nor lever. She shook one, then the other. They seemed frozen.

Alexander's smirk returned. "I shall do that for you," he said, reaching out again.

"Go. Away!" She shoved him and he stumbled, sword sheath clanging loudly against the metal of the door.

"You're on my paw!" he yelped.

"I'll stand on both of your paws if you don't move!" shouted Delphine.

A deep bang split the air. It had come from behind the door. They froze.

Then a long, low reverberation sounded, like a chain being dragged across a massive block of stone. The doors swung open. Silhouetted in front of them stood a huge badger.

The mice fell back, struck dumb.

"My children." The badger's deep voice rumbled as he stepped forward and gestured widely, the sleeves of his monk's robe hanging loose. Gold embroidery edged his cuffs and hem, and Delphine noticed a gilded design woven into the sleeves as well. Was it her imagination, or did it look a little like the crest from the linens?

"When was the last time I had guests?" His eyes were bright with pleasure. "Come in, child of Desjardins and child of Peltinore Castle."

"He knows who we are?" Delphine whispered to Alexander.

Alexander pointed to the crest that was tooled into his leather sword sheath. Then he bowed low and glided across the threshold with supreme elegance.

How does he always do that? Delphine simmered. Two seconds earlier he'd been bumbling about and quarreling with her, and now he seemed a prince.

She pulled herself together and glanced at the badger as she, too, stepped through the open door. "We thought this place was abandoned."

The badger laughed good-heartedly. "Not yet, not yet. I am still very much in residence. Father Guillaume is my name."

"How do you know I'm from Château Desjardins?"

"Come, little silver-whiskered mouse." He gestured again, and smiled at her. His fur was weathered and age-beaten, eyes nearly hidden in crinkles of laughter, the once-black bands across his face now mostly gray. Such a glow of peace emanated from his smile that she found herself smiling back.

She stepped farther into the monastery, hearing the doors

close firmly behind her. Beneath her paws was a design carved long ago into the stone floor. Despite being worn nearly smooth by centuries of paws crossing it, she thought she recognized it, too, as the crest from the linens. She would have stayed to look at it more closely, but the monk was already walking ahead.

He led them through musty, badger-size corridors and wide-open arched spaces, cavernous and silent. Cobwebs danced across ceilings, moving in breezes she could not feel. The night sky was black through the windows they passed, yet somehow the walls still glowed silver, as if the moon outside were full instead of no bigger than a sliver of cheese.

Finally, Delphine couldn't contain herself any longer. "What is this place?" she asked. "Where is that light coming from? The moon is new tonight." She faltered. "I mean . . . isn't it?"

He stopped and stared at her so intently that she squirmed and finally looked away. "Interesting," he said gently. "So you see the silvery light?"

"Don't *you*?" she responded, suddenly self-conscious.

"I do." But he left it at that, and began walking again.

At last, Delphine and Alexander spied a rectangle of yellow candlelight at the end of the corridor, and smelled the delicious aroma of something simmering over a low flame.

"Let us sup," announced Father Guillaume as they entered.

It was a cunningly designed space with a small stove and oven to heat the room and cook the meals all at once. Bits of garlic paper and parsley stems littered the counter, and a large potato rested in the corner.

Delphine loved the whole room instantly, and it deepened her fondness for the badger. Taking the needle sheath off her back, she leaned it up against the big table. She noticed Guillaume glancing at the sheath, but he merely placed two chunks of brick on the benches. "Those should be about the right height to help you reach the table, I think," he said with a chuckle. Then he turned to the stove. "I have a great affection for cooking with the greens from our garden." The badger pulled three earthen bowls from the cupboard, one large and two small. He filled each with stew from the pot bubbling on the stove. "It takes time to tend, but I always appreciate what grows there."

He set the bowls onto the rough-hewn table and produced spoons small enough for the mice. "Now sit, eat, and tell me what brings you to the monastery."

Between bites, Delphine related all that had happened, and how she had traveled to Tymbale in search of answers. She even took the needle from the sheath and showed it to Father Guillaume, before carefully stowing it away again.

When the meal was done and the story told, Father Guillaume sat for a long time, staring thoughtfully. "You . . . You prickle a memory somewhere in the corners of my mind," he said, tapping a curved claw against his temple. "Many, many years ago, so long I can barely remember, I came to this monastery as a young badger seeking training. The abbot was already ancient when I arrived. And in those days, he often told the story of a mouse who had come here long ago seeking shelter from a storm.

"Not the kind of storm that falls from the sky," he continued, rising and gathering their bowls to scrub out with clean sand. "The kind of storm with claws and teeth and knives. A storm of rats."

Delphine leaned forward, eating up every word.

"This was just before the War to End All Wars," Father Guillaume continued. "The abbot always said that was why he recalled it so clearly. It was the first he had heard of the rats' cruelty, and so when the war began in earnest a few years later, he thought back often to this mouse and wondered just how much she had known." He seemed to catch the eagerness on Delphine's face and cleared his throat. "In the abbot's story, the mouse had shown up one night, bedraggled, terrified, and clutching a human-size needle as if her life depended on it. She had begged for shelter, and they welcomed her. She told a terrifying tale of being pursued by a horde of rats who wanted to take the needle.

"The needle, she said, was not just any needle," he continued, eyes half-closed as he thought back. "It was one of the Threaded's needles. The rats had stolen it from the Threaded, and the mouse in turn had stolen it from the rats. She was determined to return it to its rightful owners. And she wanted to avenge someone. But who? I cannot recall. That was all so long ago. . . ." He wiped at his eyes and Delphine noticed how rheumy and clouded they were. She realized he was far older than she had first thought.

"How did the story end?" she asked gently.

"The mouse accepted food and shelter but then continued on her way. She knew she would bring the wrath of the rats down upon wherever she stayed, you see. I suppose she would have felt responsible if anything had happened to the monks of the monastery."

"I can understand that," Delphine said quietly. Again, she thought of Maman back at the château, and how much danger could come to her if Delphine were to send word home. And now . . . if she stayed at the monastery for too long, she might put Father Guillaume in danger as well. She was beginning to realize that there was nowhere she could safely stay, not until this quest was finished.

But Father Guillaume was still talking. "Those linens you carry," he continued. "The abbot would speak of how he gave her the cloth from the altar to wrap around the needle and hide it from sight. I never understood why he would give her an altar cloth. It is a sacred item. But now that I see the needle with my own eyes, I understand." He gestured at it in its sheath, still leaning against the table. "It, too, is a sacred item. There is something very special about it, something undeniable. I would do the same."

Delphine's head was reeling. "But *is* it the same needle?" she stammered. "How can you be sure?"

He shrugged. "I do not *know* it is the same one," he said. "I assume. I theorize. A needle of the Threaded departed this monastery once upon a time, wrapped in cloths from the altar. You were found wrapped in altar cloths of this monastery, an unusual needle alongside you. It seems likely to be the same one, does it not?"

Delphine felt the need to look at the needle again. She slid it from its sheath and placed it on the table in front of them. Father Guillaume watched. Then he asked gently, "May I hold it?"

She nodded and passed it to him. He let it rest in his great, thick paws.

"Then the real question is where the needle went for those hundred years," Alexander chimed in.

"Not to mention why it ended up with me." Delphine clenched her jaw. "And the *most* urgent question is why the rats want it so badly that they're willing to kill for it."

"They were willing to kill for it a hundred years ago, too," Alexander pointed out.

But Guillaume shook his head. "It is not so simple an answer, I think. Different rats. A different time. And why now? Why not during the hundred years between when it left the monastery and when it came to Delphine?" He turned the needle this way and that, examining the runes now visible in the silvery patch of the long, tarnished shaft.

"Maybe it was hidden somewhere," offered Alexander.

They all fell silent.

Father Guillaume placed the needle back on the table. "There was one other detail to the story," he said in his thick, husky voice. "A detail that seemed unlikely, even impossible. Until tonight." The air in the room stood still, as if the whole monastery were listening.

"Yes?" Delphine said in a small voice.

"In the abbot's story, the mouse had silver whiskers."

Delphine's paws flew to her face.

He nodded solemnly. "The abbot always said he had never seen another mouse with silver whiskers. Nor have I, in all my years."

"But I . . . my whiskers just turned silver. They were always gray."

"It happened when you held the needle in front of the tapestries!" Alexander broke in. "Maybe it was the same thing for that mouse!"

"It didn't happen to you when *you* touched it that night," Delphine pointed out.

"No!" Alexander was getting more and more excited. "That's not what I mean. Maybe it happened to you because you're the same as that mouse. Maybe . . . maybe you're related!"

"That mouse . . ." Even as she spoke, she knew in her gut that Alexander was right. "She was my ancestor?" Delphine twitched her tail excitedly. "Is that possible?"

"Anything is possible." Father Guillaume rose, pouring a

round of cordial for all of them. "And that seems *likely*. I believe that the castle mouse speaks the truth."

Delphine lapsed into thought, sipping the cordial. It was raspberry, sweet and tangy at the same time, a taste of summer in the middle of autumn.

Father Guillaume broke into his slow smile, gesturing at her cup. "I make it every year from the vines that grow wild on the grounds. I drink it on nights like this, when a little sip of sunshine gives promise to the heart that spring will come again."

"It's lovely." Delphine took another sip, then pondered the topic at hand. "Even if that mouse were my ancestor, it still doesn't help me figure out what's happening now. And my ancestor—we don't know who she was, or where she came from."

Father Guillaume tapped his claws on the table, musing. "I remember the abbot saying that she had been sent here by a music master."

"Then did the abbot send her somewhere in turn?" pressed Delphine eagerly, her hope renewed.

He shook his head slowly. "No, he had no idea where she was headed. She disappeared back into the forest and he never saw her again. The music master—I remember that detail only because the abbot often spoke of her as well. His old friend . . ." He trailed off, then glanced back down at Delphine, almost tenderly. "I suppose I always felt a kindness toward this poor little mouse in the story. When you appeared on my doorstep, it was as if time was coming back around to start again."

It was strange to Delphine as well. "It's almost like history is repeating itself." Then she focused on what Father Guillaume had just said. "This music master. Who was she?"

"Now *that* bit of information is not relegated solely to my fading memories. Her name will, in all likelihood, reside in the monastery records. Shall we go on a hunt?"

Delphine leapt up, not needing to be asked twice. Then she remembered her manners. "Thank you for dinner," she said. "It was the best meal we've had in weeks."

She looked over to Alexander to find that, against all his castle training, he had put his head down on the table and was snoring softly.

"Let him sleep. We have a name to find." Guillaume placed one giant paw on her shoulder. "He has a strong heart and a gentle soul. Take care of him, and he will take care of you."

She twitched her nose. "I don't need taking care of."

"Everyone needs taking care of, child." Father Guillaume turned to pick up a nearby beeswax candle in its holder. After lighting it at the fire under the stewpot, he began to slowly lumber back down the dark hallway. "Come, and we shall search for your answers."

They traveled through winding corridors and finally reached a wide oak door that opened with a sigh, revealing a massive shelf-lined library. The badger-size books were stored in rows, with shelves rising up toward the vaulted ceiling. Long, spindly ladders leaned here and there to allow access to the upper shelves. Clearly, Father Guillaume visited this room regularly, given how dust-free and organized the books remained.

Guillaume used the beeswax candle to light a row of tapers, illuminating the library in a soft yellow glow. Delphine tiptoed down the rows, touching tome after tome of ancient history. She noticed they were mostly made of delicate vellum or onion-paper, bound together by thread and dried snail slime. The spines were worn, handled by centuries of paws, but still legible. Painted gold curlicues called out names and dates long gone: *Belltower Upkeep 1627–1649*; *Belltower Upkeep 1650–1673*. *Bran Petite-Oreille, The Tail Of* sat alongside *Bran Petite-Oreille, The Teachings Of.* Farther down, a whole series of *Grain & Legume Crops* took up three entire rows, each labeled with the moon and year. There was a world of information here, and no time to even begin to absorb it.

The sound of the badger clearing his throat brought her attention to the front of the hall. He was holding a fragile folio bound in scarlet leather faded by the years to dusky brown. She scurried back to him and stood on tiptoe to read the cover. His age-scarred claws obscured some of the lettering, but she could still make out the title: *Concerts & Musical Performances: Main Abbey: 1672–1714.*

Delphine followed Father Guillaume to a nearby wooden stand, which had clearly been hand carved, and polished many times over the years. He placed the folio upon it. "Record keeping has always been one of the prides of Tymbale." He turned the loose-leaf pages carefully. Then he paused. "Look here," he said, and tapped the copperplate writing with one of his massive claws.

Delphine peered at the page. It seemed just the same as the others. The handwriting was so crabbed that she could barely make out a single word. Then she noticed a name written several times in swooping flourishes. A different paw altogether had made that notation, almost like an incantation.

"*Speranta del Allegretti Fortencio*," she read slowly, sounding out the name.

"The very same. Signed in her own hand, as was the habit of the time. Accomplished visitors were often asked to sign our ledgers as a special honor." Guillaume leaned over the book closely, and for a moment it seemed as if Speranta's signature shimmered silver across the page.

Delphine rubbed her eyes surreptitiously and stifled a yawn.

Guillaume, head still bent over the book, said, "We have found the name. And so now I think it is time for you to head to bed."

"I'm not tired," she insisted half-heartedly.

"Nor is the moon when it is her turn to rest," Guillaume responded cryptically. He copied the name down onto a loose scrap of vellum and placed it in her paw. "Take care. The ink is still wet."

She stood, looking at his spidery writing while he lumbered down the rows to return the folio to its proper place. "This music master, Speranta del Allegretti Fortencio . . ." she started when he had returned. "Where was her school?" As tired as she was, her mind was already planning ahead. They could leave immediately—uncover who that visiting mouse was, and why she'd had that needle. It might not answer her larger questions about her own past, but it would be another step in the right direction.

"We shall discuss it in the morning," he replied. He blew out the tapers and headed back down the hallway.

Delphine trotted after him, gripping the vellum scrap. "But we have the name! This is half the puzzle!" As exhausted as she was, she couldn't imagine doing anything but pushing forward to unravel the secrets of the needle.

"My child," came the badger's low voice in front of her. "Do you plan to continue your journey at this very moment, while night still hangs above us?"

"Well . . ." Delphine hadn't really thought about it that way. Granted, the new moon was rising, but so were the owls and ferrets and bats and all the other denizens of the night world. She had to admit, it felt nice to be somewhere cozy after so much time sleeping on dirt and under leaves. "I suppose not."

As he showed her into a clever little room made up with a

walnut-shell bed and a woven rope rug, she still had one burning question. "You never told me why the walls glow."

Guillaume gave her the same curious look he had laid upon her earlier. She winced, wondering if she should have held her tongue.

Then he smiled widely. "You mentioned the moonlight earlier. But not the walls. I was wondering how long you would wait to ask."

What?

"The moon does not shine solely from the sky." With that, Guillaume closed the door gently, leaving her alone. His heavy tread receded down the corridor, and then all was quiet.

Delphine glanced around at the simple wooden table and stool, the little vase made of a human thimble, the neatly drawn damask curtain. Her head was spinning. What had he meant? How had he known she would ask? And this music master, this Speranta . . .

She fumbled in her apron and pulled out the scrap of vellum. As soon as day broke, she would set back out on the road to follow this next clue, to see if she could find any more information about the old music school connected to her ancestor. She wouldn't rest until she had discovered why the mouse had stolen the needle from the rats, and why the rats had had a needle of the Threaded in the first place. But for now, she needed something to distract her thoughts. Her eye fell on a frayed rip in the corner of the comforter. She could stitch that up for Father Guillaume as a little merci for his kindness.

Clambering into bed, Delphine pulled the comforter toward her, drawing out the loose threads. It would be easy enough to weave them back together. But the dandelion fluff was soft as a cloud. Her eyelids were drooping against her will. She could feel herself drifting.

Between one breath and the next, sleep took her.

Interlude

"*Y*ou *witless fool! Curse the day you came to work in my kitchen!*"
*Another pot came flying at Rien's head. He ducked and the pot crashed
into a stack of clean plates being dried by one of the other kitchen rats.*

*"Idiot!" The rat with the drying rag came barreling across the kitchen—
at Rien, instead of his attacker. Rien was always the target, whether or not
it was his fault. He cried out, wrapping his paws around his head to protect
his ears, and the rat cracked him on the snout. The mice working on the prep*

line snickered as they chopped vegetables, not bothering to intervene. Rien ducked under the table and dashed out the back door into the yard. He knew he'd be punished later for running, but he didn't care.

When he was certain nobody had followed him, he climbed up into his favorite hiding place, a dusty little hole above the stables. He hugged himself tightly to keep from crying. He could hear the stablehands outside, driving a herd of beetles out to pasture.

When he felt a little better, Rien unwrapped his arms and examined his wounds. He licked his paw and touched it to his ear, wincing at the pain. Another fresh burn, probably from that pot as it had whizzed past.

It wasn't just the other rats who picked on him. Many of the mice who worked in the kitchen or stables would kick him for fun, a way to make themselves feel better. "A rat who's smaller than we are," they would joke to one another. "Let's be sure he stays that way, eh, mates?"

Rien gazed through a crack in the wall, out at the bright sunshine on the rocks below. Why did everyone have to be so cruel? Even the mice? He sighed, telling himself the same thing he always did: They don't realize that they're being cruel. Life is hard for all of us.

He spotted Elodie crossing the rocks, and his heart soared. She was still the only one in the whole fortress who had ever been kind to him. How had she known that he needed her? She always seemed to know. He pulled out his red handkerchief and stuffed it partway through the crack, their signal that he was in his hiding place. He saw her glance up, then look over at the main buildings. Checking to be sure nobody saw where she was headed, he assumed.

 157

He went back to carefully cleaning his ear where it had been burned. A few minutes later, he heard a light step on the hidden ladder, and then Elodie's little head popped in through the cutout in the wood.

"Rien!" she gasped, catching sight of his wounds.

He managed a lopsided grin. "Hello, Elodie."

She ran to him and pressed her delicate paws against his rough snout.

"I'm all right."

Her touch was cool against the still-smarting bruise. "You poor thing," she murmured. "They're always picking on you. I wish I could do something about it."

"Really, it's not as bad as it looks. I'm just glad you're here. Did you bring more pebbles for our game? I saw you out on the rocks."

Her face lit up. "I did!" Elodie dug in her basket and produced a handful of smooth, round pebbles from the riverbank. He was already digging out the gameboard he had made from a discarded baking pan. He carefully arranged the pebbles they already had, and she added the new ones.

"Who moves first?" she asked, and he pointed at her.

The time passed quickly as it always did when they were together. Too quickly. Before they knew it, they could hear the dinner bell being rung. "I'm late!" Elodie leapt up, spilling pebbles everywhere.

She knelt back down to help Rien gather them, but he grinned at her and pushed her paws away. "You're always late. Go." Elodie returned the smile and grabbed her basket, disappearing down the ladder.

Rien carefully piled the stones in a neat little stack. Soon enough, he would have to return to the kitchen, but he decided to stay long enough to watch the sun set. Curling up in a little nest of hay, he stared out through the crack. Just a few minutes more. The hay was warm, and he was so tired. In the blink of an eye, Rien was asleep.

Chapter 10

Delphine was awakened by the sound of fighting. She leapt out of the bed and tripped on the corner of the woven rope rug, nearly falling over. Pulling herself to her feet, she grabbed the needle, rushed from the room, and ran pell-mell down the halls. Had the rats found them?

She skidded around a corner, frantic and thoroughly lost. Then she caught a waft of fresh-baked bread in the air, along with another defiant shout. She doubled back and raced toward the sounds until she saw the arched doorway of the kitchen ahead. She could hear Alexander shouting "Stand back!" and the ring of his sword against metal.

Fear mounting, Delphine skidded through the doorway, ready to take on the unknown villain and rescue Alexander . . . who, in fact, was standing on the table, mouth full of croissant, enthusiastically dueling with a hanging pot as Guillaume nodded with interest.

"Hawkworms, everywhere!" Alexander was squeaking. "There I was, with just a penknife, and wearing my finest ruby-encrusted justeaucorps and breeches. That whole ensemble, by the way"—he made a swoosh in the air with the croissant clutched in his other paw—"had been constructed from the most elaborate brocade ever seen in court. Designed just for me, of course. Did I mention the rubies? Sewn all over the justeaucorps, even on the pocket flaps, quite unlike anything attempted before. What a glorious picture I cut that day."

Delphine slumped against the doorway. Unbelievable. There she had been, ready to snatch him from the jaws of disaster, and he was regaling Guillaume with that stupid hawkworm story. Poor Father Guillaume.

"Alexander. I'm so pleased to see you slept well last night," Delphine said crisply. She was about to turn to greet Father Guillaume when she noticed Alexander staring at her with a grin.

"Your whiskers are absolutely frizzled on that side," he said, pointing at her left cheek. "You really should spend more time on your morning ablutions."

Delphine's nostrils flared. That was the last straw. "You!" she yelled. "You pass out on the dinner table like a commoner, then you bore Father Guillaume with your tall tales, and now you mock me?"

"At least I'm not running frantically around the halls at half morning."

He was so smug, it made Delphine's eyeteeth hurt. She refocused on Father Guillaume, who winked at her good-naturedly.

"You were both rather tired. The sleep of the well-traveled walker is the deepest sleep indeed." He popped a wheat grain into his mouth and bit down, cracking the shell. "Speaking of which, I returned to the library this morning and located the name of the music school you seek."

Delphine's mouth dropped open. "You did?"

"The old Fortencio Académie was located in Parfumoisson. Perhaps you'll be able to find what remains of it there." He pulled out a large square of vellum covered in carefully drawn mountains, rivers, and towns. "I have prepared this map to assist in your travels."

Delphine felt positively ashamed of her behavior. She thought of what Maman would say about her running through the halls and then bickering with a noblemouse in front of such a kind host. "Thank you," she choked, taking the map from the badger.

She spotted Tymbale Monastery, inked in careful detail with a rendering of Fox Rock nearby. A dotted line led north and then west along a river to the coast that held Parfumoisson— evidently where the Fortencio Académie had once been.

Guillaume patted the chunk of brick on the bench next to him, and she climbed up onto it sheepishly. "I used to spend several months of each year traveling through the lands of Peltinore," he told her. "I am secure in my belief that I have given you the best route."

"Thank you," Delphine said again, now blushing even harder. "You did all this while I was sleeping?"

Guillaume smiled. "Sleep is always a worthy endeavor." Then his face grew serious. "You may not have as much time for it on the road. You must be always aware, on guard, watching to keep one another safe. The rats of this kingdom have been power and magic hungry for the last century. They will stop at nothing to get that needle."

✳ ✳ ✳

After breakfast, the two mice packed their meager belongings. The map fit neatly inside the needle sheath, and Delphine stored the scrap of vellum with Speranta's name in her apron pocket. She was eager to get back on the road but found herself sad to leave Father Guillaume.

The badger handed them bags filled with dried foods and

supplies, which Delphine and Alexander gratefully accepted. Then he walked with them to the edge of the overgrown gardens. The smell of the last honeysuckle blossoms lay rich in the air. Delphine glanced toward the crumbling wall surrounding the grounds, and the dark and foreboding woods beyond. If the rats were to have followed her here . . .

She turned to Father Guillaume. "Will *you* be safe?"

He patted her shoulder reassuringly. "Worry not, little mowse. I've survived this long. And Tymbale is not so easily reached by those who are less than true of heart."

Delphine nodded as he stepped forward to join Alexander, chatting with the noblemouse in a low voice. A thought suddenly occurred to her. Scooping up a handful of dry dirt from the garden bed, she knotted it into a corner of her cloak. Now she would be able to powder her silver whiskers whenever they crossed paths with others.

Guillaume and Alexander finished talking, and Alexander began scaling the wall. Meanwhile, the monk knelt beside Delphine. "May I examine your needle one last time?"

She slipped it from its sheath and handed it to him. *Your* needle, she noticed he had said. Not *the* needle.

Turning it over so that the morning sun glinted off the engravings, he began to speak. The light filled her eyes, and his voice filled her mind in such a way that, later, while she could never recall quite what he had said, she could have sworn she had understood it deep in her bones.

Guillaume placed her needle back into her paws, and the spell was broken. "Find the start, Delphine. To unravel any mystery, find the start. Untie that riddle, and the rest will follow."

Delphine thought of her mother's similar advice: *Find the knot.* She nodded, resolute. And after bidding the badger a heartfelt good-bye, she joined Alexander.

The morning air was crisp and quiet, broken only by the call of a sparrow in the distance. The soft, loamy dirt would make it easy to walk. They turned their tails to Tymbale, their noses to the north. Rested and fed, they headed once more into the unknown.

the chaumes moon

Chapter 11

The Chaumes moon was already well on its way to being full before Delphine and Alexander had even reached the river marked on Guillaume's map.

Between them, they had suffered three splinters (Delphine), a torn ear (also Delphine), several raw toe pads (yet again Delphine), and a temporary discoloration of a left front claw (Alexander, after attempting to show off how he could balance a mulberry on his claw despite Delphine's warnings that mulberry juice was used to stain fabrics). So Delphine was not feeling particularly kindly when Alexander complained about one of his hind paws aching.

"You have boots," she pointed out for what felt like the thousandth time. "I don't, and I'm not complaining. Anyway, soon enough we'll be on the river, and then we won't need shoes at all."

Alexander sat down on a large pebble and began to undo his shoefly wing laces. "I'm just not particularly fond of water travel," he muttered. He pulled off his boot and shook out a few minuscule specks of dirt.

Delphine folded her arms. "What are you saying? That you're not coming with me on the river? If it's too much for you, maybe you should go back to the castle."

"You know I'm not going back." Alexander was clearly miffed now, too. "I've taken an oath to protect you." He pulled back on his ant-skin boot, hopping around in a most inelegant fashion as he wiggled it all the way back onto his paw.

Seems like I'm the one protecting you most of the time, she wanted to say, but she resisted the urge. "Well, why *did* you take that oath to protect me?"

Alexander squinted at the sky. "You really want to know the truth?"

"*Yes!*"

"The castle is so terribly dull," he said, turning up his nose. "I figured if I went on a quest at least I could get a little adventure in my life."

"Come on," she said with a sigh, not wanting to admit that she'd had similar feelings before that fateful castle letter had arrived at her doorstep. Though of course, that was before her life depended on completing said quest. She headed toward the river's edge. Alexander fell into step behind her, still lacing his boot as he went.

Most of the travelers seemed to be crossing the river, rather than traveling up or down it. A frog was poling back and forth in a wooden human bowl, taking paying passengers across the water. Alexander sniffed at the sight of the wooden bowl with its endless rotation of animals. "How filthy it must be—" he began, but he caught a glimpse of Delphine folding her arms, and he had the sense to stop his sentence in its tracks. "Anyway, we can't ride in that even if we wanted to," he amended. "We need to go downstream, don't we?"

Delphine nodded, staring hard at one particularly long-nosed stoat hanging around the edge of the crowd. She didn't like his weevily looks, or how he seemed to be eyeing the purses tied on most passengers' belts. She glanced at Alexander. "Do you see—?" But by the time she looked back at the crowd, the stoat was gone.

"What?" Alexander looked up, retying his boots for the third time in order to get the bows perfectly aligned.

She rolled her eyes. "Never mind."

Then Delphine noticed a group of newts hanging around idly on the shore. Tall and lanky, they were garbed in a bizarre hodge-podge of garments, each less fashionable than the last. More importantly, they were standing in front of a sign offering skiffs for rent to those brave enough to be traveling along the river.

Then Delphine got a closer look at the skiffs themselves. They were crumbling where they sat, moldy piles of driftwood barely lashed together with frayed bits of discarded cord. She shook her head in disbelief. But it seemed to be their only option.

Delphine glanced at Alexander, then back down the muddy hill. A plan was coming together. "I'm going to go find out how much they charge for one of those hole-filled embarrassments. Stay here until I call you." She pulled a pinch of dry dirt out of the knot in her cloak and rubbed it into her whiskers, dulling the silver shine as best she could.

Alexander looked doubtful. "And what will we do with one of those? Do you know anything at all about boats?"

Delphine nodded briskly. "There's a little pond near our château. I know enough to keep us afloat." She strode down the steep hill, deftly stepping through the mud. "Just watch for my signal!" she called over her shoulder.

"Wait!" Alexander cried. "They're common crooks, by the looks of them! They'll charge you a leg and a tail! And we don't even have anything to barter with in the first place! Delphine, stop!"

But she had already reached the newts. "Gentlemen, what a pleasure." Delphine dipped into her best curtsey, then straightened up with as much Alexander-style aplomb as she could muster. "I couldn't help but notice that you all are connoisseurs of fashion."

The newt who seemed to be the leader of the gang gave a throaty chuckle. "That we are, miss. We be the Courant Boys."

"The *Au* Courant Boys!" piped up one of the younger newts, and was rewarded with a smack upside the head.

"Quit tellin' my joke before me!" snapped the leader. Then he turned back to Delphine, a slimy grin oozing across his face. "Lookin' for a water vehicle, perchance? If so, then I, Alphonse-Bertrand, am at your service."

She nodded as innocently as she could. "Why yes, indeed. And we can offer you some courtly garments in exchange."

"I should think so, a well-dressed pair like you two." Alphonse-Bertrand leered up the hill behind her.

She spun around. Sure enough, Alexander was heading down toward them. She sighed. He just couldn't follow simple instructions, could he? She would have to speed things up. "I see you have no *headwear*," she whispered to the lead newt, hoping to make it seem like such an embarrassing situation that she couldn't even speak of it aloud.

"Delph—" Alexander began to call, forgetting to look down as he placed his paw. The mud enveloped his boot instantly and he tumbled headlong. He slid down the hill, flailing, boots flying, finally coming to a stop at the feet of the newts.

Delphine stared down at him with the look of distaste

typically reserved for a bit of unpleasant vegetable stalk found in the midst of a delicious cassoulet.

"Gentlemen," Alexander said as if nothing were amiss. He nodded to each of them in turn from where he lay in the mud.

Delphine poked him sharply in the ribs with her toe. "Alexander, I was just about to trade your cap to this fine fellow here, but you seem to have lost it."

He peeled himself genteelly upward to a standing position. "My cap? My velvet cap with the bluebird feather?" He reached upward, and Delphine stared pointedly at the ground behind him. He swiveled around and plucked the bedraggled lump of velvet out of the mud.

Delphine gritted her teeth, her mind racing furiously. How was she going to salvage this? Another idea sprang into her head. Scurrying over, she lifted the cap from Alexander's paws and trotted to the river. "Thank goodness it's not Drizellan velvet," she announced as she rinsed it in the rushing water. "Then it really would be ruined."

Alexander was aghast. "What? I'll have you know that cap is made of the finest velvet in all of Peltinore!" He drew himself up to his full height.

"My point exactly," she volleyed as she gave the cap a final swish and then carefully pulled it out of the water. It looked like a drowned marshfly. She traipsed back over to the group of newts with the cap in her paw. "This is no cheap Drizellan velvet. This is the finest *Cinderellan* velvet, straight from the kingdom of, ah . . . Lucifee. Only the best velvet can go through mud and water and come out looking even better than when it went in. You, my good sir, are tremendously lucky that my courtly friend has only the finest taste in fabrics."

Alphonse-Bertrand looked unconvinced, his shiny eyes staring unblinking at her.

Delphine gave the cap a few quick twists to wring out the water, and placed it with gravitas on top of Alexander's head. "Would you not agree that in fact the cap is now even more charming than before?"

While Alphonse-Bertrand still seemed skeptical, the rest of the newts were nodding to one another now, impressed. "Cinderellan velvet," said one. "I've heard of it, you know."

Delphine collected their travel bags from where Alexander had dropped them, then began to hustle Alexander toward the closest skiff. "Put these in there and get on board," she hissed under her breath.

Alexander looked at the boat, then back at her. "But we haven't—"

"Go!" Delphine flicked her eyes at the nearest skiff once more. As he turned, she grabbed the cap back off his head.

"My cap!" he yelped. Reaching for it, he slipped in the mud, tumbling forward into the boat and landing on one of the seating planks. Luckily, Delphine noted, the sacks went into the boat with him.

She turned back to the clump of newts, now all gabbling

enthusiastically. She addressed Alphonse-Bertrand directly. "If you're not interested in this trade, my good newt, I'm sure that one of your colleagues will be?"

Several of them stepped forward, clamoring excitedly.

"No!" Alphonse-Bertrand snatched the cap from her paws and jammed it down on his head.

Delphine smiled. Nothing like the fear of slipping a notch on the social ladder to inspire greediness. She curtseyed again. "Monsieur. Such a pleasure."

Alphonse-Bertrand beamed from ear to ear. "Enjoy your ride," he said snidely. She could tell he thought he was getting the better end of the deal.

Delphine leapt lightly into the skiff. "Au revoir!" she called merrily as they began to push back from the shore into the swiftly flowing waters. She turned to look at Alexander. At that moment, the skiff jolted beneath her.

She spun around and her blood turned to ice. Alphonse-Bertrand had grabbed the rope trailing from the aft and was pulling them back toward shore. He seemed to be yelling something, but his words were drowned out by the river.

Delphine cupped a paw around her ear, trying to act unconcerned, but her heart was in her throat. What could they do? Leap off the boat? Try to swim to the other side? Could Alexander even swim?

Alphonse-Bertrand bellowed louder. "Just wanted to say

merci beaucoup once again! It's not often I get to do business with mice from another kingdom!"

Delphine smiled weakly, her heart pounding.

The newt dropped the rope and waved as the skiff began to drift into the center of the current. The rest of the bunch swarmed around him, jabbering over who could borrow the cap first. Their voices were quickly drowned out once more by the rushing river.

As they moved away from the shore, Delphine again had the funniest feeling that she was being watched. *Was it the strange stoat again?* But she blinked and only saw the tree-lined shore. Delphine rubbed her eyes. She must be delirious after so long on the road.

Alexander turned toward her. "That cap was ruined!"

Delphine shrugged. "Beauty is in the eye of the beholder."

"Beauty was that cap before you dunked it in the river. And what in the world is 'Drizellan velvet'? And 'Cinderellan velvet'?"

She shrugged again. "How should I know?"

His mouth fell open. "Do you mean . . . ?"

She smiled.

Alexander struggled to compose himself. "But—"

"They'll never know anything other than that they're now the owners of an extremely fashionable cap, straight from the courts of Lucifee, wherever that is. Besides, this thing they call a boat isn't worth anything at all. It was a fair trade, when all was said and done."

He leaned back, disbelieving. "Where did that all come from?"

Delphine gave a sly grin. "Let's just say that I've been listening to someone tell a lot of tall tales for quite a few weeks now." And before Alexander could respond, she nipped to the front of the skiff and began poling energetically downstream.

After a few minutes, Delphine realized Alexander had not lied—water travel did *not* suit him. She watched his ears grow more and more tinged with green, and by the time they had found a reed midriver to tie on to for the night, he was refusing any nourishment at all.

"Not a single morsel of walnut?" pressed Delphine, nibbling from one of the packets that Father Guillaume had prepared for them. Alexander just groaned and buried his head in his paws.

✳ ✳ ✳

With every passing day, the flow of the river lessened. Time seemed to pass more slowly, too, with little for them to do but mend and organize their meager supplies. Delphine patched the spots that had rubbed thin in the fabric of their travel bags, and then she started patching the multitude of holes in the old canvases that had come with the skiff. She spent several hours retying all the dilapidated cords that were holding most of the boat together. The wood itself was so worm-eaten and sun battered that it looked like it would crumble if it hit a rock too hard, so they took turns sitting at the prow, keeping a pole's length away from any oncoming rocks in their path.

Delphine also found herself bringing the needle out from its sheath more and more, resting it on her lap and running her paw across the engravings. She could feel the needle fizzing with energy, just as it had in the hidden room of tapestries, almost as if it had been woken up by the touch of her paw under the moonlight. She wondered if the fresh air was continuing to charge it somehow.

Once, as she gazed at the needle, the engraving shimmered beneath her touch. She leaned closer and closer until Alexander caught sight of her and cleared his throat worriedly. Then the trance broke and she sat back up, but the light-headedness stayed for hours, like the last remnants of a fading headache.

The river soon slowed to a lazy flow. During the days, the sun would sit high in the sky, and they could enjoy a few minutes of relative warmth before the ever-lengthening chilly evenings. The riverbanks rolled by, an endless panoply of bushes and tree roots and pebbly sand. Every time Delphine looked at Father Guillaume's map, she wished she could tell how far along the river they had traveled. All she knew was that day by day, autumn was passing much too quickly. They wouldn't be able to survive on their own once the snow came. She had to solve this riddle soon.

"We have to be getting close to the river's mouth," said Alexander for the thousandth time, as he attempted to mend a rip in his waistcoat.

"The princess's own dressmaker isn't good enough to repair your garments?" she said mildly from her perch at the stern. Her needle rested in her paws, as had become her habit.

"I'm not *completely* inept," Alexander tossed back. He tried yet again to weave the two sides of the rip together, but the fabric slipped from his paws. He grimaced, then set it aside.

"I should mend your jacket with *this* needle," she teased. "Can you imagine that? Sewing with this oversize thing? Two stitches and the whole thing would be complete." She gestured grandly in the air with her needle as she spoke, pretending to make oversize stitches. "Jacket . . . mended!"

A shower of silvery light erupted from the tip of her needle. The sparks sprayed across the stern and sizzled as they hit the water around them.

Delphine squeaked, throwing her needle into the bottom of the boat, where it rolled to a stop. It lay motionless and silent.

Alexander was frozen, eyes huge. "What just happened?"

Delphine swallowed her shock and reached out one paw to prod her needle. Nothing.

"I don't know," she whispered. She picked it up and waved it from side to side. Still nothing.

"You said something right before it happened," Alexander hissed.

"Why are you whispering?" she whispered back, still holding her needle at paw's length like a live hawkworm.

"You're whispering, too!"

Delphine cleared her throat. "I was saying," she started clearly and slowly, trying to remain calm, "that I would repair your jacket." She waved her needle through the air again. A few bits of silvery light flickered from the tip and fizzled out. This time, Delphine did not let go.

"It's a magic wand!" came Alexander's hushed voice.

"Stop whispering!" Delphine demanded. "It's not that scary!" She felt she had to approach this head-on. "And it's not a magic wand. Those only exist in fairy tales." She waved the needle like a magic wand anyway. No luck.

Delphine tried furiously to remember. What exactly *had* she been doing? She struggled to recall how it had felt. Like a bolt of lightning springing from . . . from where?

Delphine spent the rest of the afternoon waving the needle this way and that, trying to get it to produce more sparks. But the harder she tried, the more lifeless it felt in her paws. Fed up, she finally shoved it out of sight.

That night, the air was still and cold. As usual, they had tied their painter line to a reed near the banks, out of the main current. The water lapped quietly at the sides of the boat.

The needle in her paws, Delphine lay with her nose poking

through a gap in the canvases, staring up at the stars. She could hear Alexander in the prow, snoring softly. Delphine counted the sounds around her, a habit she had learned in childhood, when her mother rubbed her temples during headaches and helped her focus on what existed beyond the pain. *What can you hear?* Maman would say, and Delphine would answer, *I can hear the wind in the trees, Cinderella singing downstairs in the kitchen, soup bubbling on the stove, the sparrows cooing in their tower nest* . . . and then she would fall asleep.

Delphine listened now, trying to distract herself from all that was running round inside her head. She heard the rustle of the air through the reeds. A night lark calling in the distance. Fish splashing. The wood of the skiff creaking softly as it swayed. Her own breathing. The stars sliding through the night sky above her. Moonlight dripping off the leaves of the trees and dappling the water in tiny silver droplets. She caught her breath. She was *hearing* stars and moonlight?

But as soon as Delphine stopped to think about it, the sounds began to fade so rapidly that she had only a moment to let herself fall back into the half trance. Fall she did, and the sounds came roiling back around her like the rush of water through a parted dam. Yes, she could hear the stars singing in low, sweet tones as they moved along their smoothly oiled paths through the sky. And the moonlight, not just dappling the water but also flowing into the land around her like silver honey, filling the trees and the sky and her whole body with its power. The moonlight started singing, too, deep and rich, and its song vibrated through her.

Delphine felt her needle growing warm, and the air around it began to shimmer. She nearly started to think again but let go just in time, and remained floating in the moment. Her needle grew warmer and warmer with each breath that she took. It seemed as if all the world were in perfect harmony, all the threads aligned. She could reach out and undo any one of them, then create a whole new pattern. The needle started to burn against her paws. She cried out, but the cry was made up of words she had never heard before, and they came out as silvery light. The light streamed around the needle, and the tarnish began to swirl once more. A bit more of the inscription began to glow.

Without knowing how or why, Delphine was standing upright in the boat, Alexander still sound asleep. She inhaled, and all the sounds of the surrounding world ceased. She was suspended in a single moment. The starsong went on, and as the moonlight flowed through her, she brought her needle slicing through the air in a series of loops and swirls that felt as if they had been written before time began. Silver light streamed from the needle, and she drew symbols in the air. The light curled and spiraled around her. Delphine glanced down and noticed that the tarnish was continuing to fade. She dove further into the silvery feeling inside her, and the light divided and divided again into glowing coils.

Then the coils burrowed down through the wood and water. Delphine felt the energy pulling away from her, growing out of control. She struggled to draw it back, but it was too late. It was too strong. The needle bucked in her paw. She watched in horror as the silvery coils kept bending and looping upon themselves, drawing tighter each time as they twisted, crushing everything they held. They tore through the wooden keel, ripping the little boat from stem to stern in an instant.

A surging wave rushed upon the mice, and they were thrown into the river. Cold water filled Delphine's nose and mouth. The spell broke, the world crashed back upon her, and then she was fighting against the current as it dragged her down to the bottom.

Needle still in her grip, Delphine thrashed, fighting her way back up to the river's surface. The skiff had become little more than a wreck of matchsticks, half its fragments caught in the reeds, the other half already whisked away by the current.

"Alexander!" Delphine screamed, water filling her mouth. "Alexander!" She flailed in the dark river, scanning the empty surface. Terror filled her. In that moment, silvery strands twisted from the needle and streamed through the water. Too panicked to wonder what was happening, she dove after them. Down, down, down she swam, until the silver strands twirling from the needle led her to the river bottom. There she saw a small, limp figure caught in a tangle of underwater roots. *Alexander!*

Delphine pulled at the roots, then stabbed at them with her needle in desperation. The roots broke apart. She grabbed the noblemouse and kicked back toward the surface. When she broke through to the air, the water was roiling around them. Pulling Alexander, Delphine headed for the shore, needle still in her other paw. Alexander was a leaden weight, and when she glanced back, she saw he wasn't stirring.

Just one more tail's-length, she told herself over and over as she swam, but it seemed as if she were barely moving against the current.

The water fell away in front of her, and a great black stone reared up. No, not a stone. A *head*. A massive head with huge, flat eyes. The jaws of the great, scaly pike fish opened and she could see past rows of sharp fangs into a maw that seemed to go on forever. She shrieked and paddled madly backward.

The pike was above her now, its body lifting out of the water as it arched back, ready to snatch them. Keeping Alexander's arm in one paw, she held the needle before her. As the pike came down, the needle leapt up like a silver dart, piercing the pike between its gleaming eyes, deep through its scales. The pike shuddered once. Delphine yanked back the needle and dove, pulling Alexander with her under the surface. She felt the crash of the pike slamming back down into the water.

When she looked up, Delphine could see the pike's massive limp body floating above them, seeming to fill the surface of the river and block all hope of escape. But she had to try. Lungs bursting, she yanked at Alexander as she fought her way past the fallen pike toward the shore.

Delphine never knew how she made it. She dragged herself onto the pebbly sand, gasping, with Alexander motionless by her side. Finally, she willed herself to move. She pressed hard on his chest, over and over, as she had seen a pond mouse do once on a pinkie who had fallen out of a boat.

"Alexander, please wake up!" Delphine pleaded with him, her voice raw. "Wake up!" His eyes were sealed shut, his whiskers wilted. She pressed again, harder, but still he did not breathe.

Delphine felt a lump form in her throat. She looked up at the moon, tears springing to her eyes. What had she done? She pounded her fists against his chest. "I'm not giving up on you!"

Alexander coughed.

Delphine gasped as the whole river seemed to come out of his mouth. She cried then, and her head fell down on his chest as he rolled to the side and retched.

"No such thing as magic?" he managed to croak.

SNURLEAU HAD WATCHED THE TWO mice set off down the river. He had noticed glimmers of the silvery whiskers peeking through crude, muddy powder . . . and the human-size needle the castle rat had described. All in a skiff so worm-rotted it would fall apart before they made it a day downstream. Snurleau couldn't resist gloating a little. This would be his easiest job yet under King Midnight's employ.

Before the skiff had drifted from view, Snurleau had been studying the other mouse with her, trying to place him. A noblemouse from the castle? Now, as he slipped back into the forest toward his next destination, the face clicked in his memory. Snurleau's lips curled back to reveal his fangs. Alexander de Soucy Perrault, that horrid noblemouse. Snurleau knew Alexander all too well. It was Alexander's fault that he had been thrown in jail in that nasty town at the base of the castle, simply because he had swiped the purse of gold pieces Alexander was collecting for an orphanage. Who collected for charity at a card game anyway? Snurleau ground his teeth at the thought. The only good thing that had come out of being thrown in jail was meeting those rats that worked for King Midnight.

Feeling more motivated than ever, Snurleau licked his lips with his sharp tongue and moved toward the road, peeking through the foliage. He'd send a message back to King Midnight, letting him know that he'd located the needle. Then he could relax and enjoy himself until Midnight sent reinforcements. And after that . . . if a certain mouse named Alexander de Soucy Perrault just happened to fall into trouble, well, these things happened.

Chapter 12

The half-drowned mice huddled in front of a makeshift fire that Delphine had managed to start. Night was slowly fading into the dim gray light of early morning.

"What happened?" Alexander asked, when his teeth had finally stopped chattering.

Delphine told him about the needle, the moonlight, the magic. She showed him how another symbol on the shaft had been revealed as the tarnish faded, though the rest was still as gray and dull as before.

Alexander didn't take her explanation well. "You were mucking around with that thing in the middle of the night?! You nearly got us both killed!"

Delphine's whiskers twitched. "I said I was sorry." She realized she truly meant it. Alexander might be a fop, but she had never meant to put him in danger.

Alexander hopped up and started pacing along the shore. "How did that happen? What did you wake up inside that needle? Could it happen again?" His questions came hard and fast.

She hurried to join him. "Exactly! Now that we know the needle really *is* magic, I can start to—"

"No!" He cut her off. "I'm saying just the opposite. You don't know what that thing truly is! You have no idea where it came from, or how to use it!"

"That's why I need to *learn* how! I know it's risky, but it might be the key to everything. At the very least, it might be useful to us in some way."

Alexander was still talking. ". . . and I wasn't even awake to make sure you were safe—"

Delphine's brow furrowed. "Because *you* always have to be the one to save *me*, is that it?" she retaliated, her tail lashing from side to side.

He stopped in midpace. "Well, yes," he said matter-of-factly. "That's the oath that I took."

"You are the most self-aggrandizing, pompous mouse that I've ever had the misfortune to know!" Delphine snapped, her remorse quickly evaporating. She grabbed the needle from where it lay on the shore and stomped into the forest. She had no idea where she was going and frankly, she didn't care. *Let him find his own way back to court where he can spend the rest of his days worrying about doublet ribbons and how to dance the gavotte*, she thought. She had to solve the mystery of this needle or she was going to spend the rest of her days on the run from rats who wanted to kill her.

I just have to figure out how I made the magic happen, and how to do it again . . . safely. Delphine headed deeper into the trees. *Besides*, she thought, *aren't I a seamstress?* She'd been using mouse-size sewing needles ever since she could remember, and she knew how to wield those needles to create beautiful things. How hard could it really be to control *this* needle, now that she had unlocked its power? Perhaps weaving threads of fabric together and weaving a magic spell might not be so different, now that she had taken the first steps.

An owl hooted in the morning stillness and Delphine froze as she looked up. In a moment, she saw it flapping slowly across the sky, its wings silent in the gray air. She shivered. The forest floor was ice-cold beneath her paws.

What in the world was she doing? Storming off into the

middle of nowhere, without a single idea where she was headed? Though she'd only walked a few tail's-lengths into the forest, she was already losing her bearings. The trees were older and broader here than they were in the south of the kingdom. The thick branches arching overhead made the early-morning light dim and diffuse. Even once the sun rose, she wouldn't be able to see it through such dense branches, so there'd be no way to know if she was still heading west. Delphine turned from side to side nervously. Everything looked the same, except her paw-prints behind her.

Nutmegs. She was going to have to keep following the river after all. She turned and headed back, sighing. It was probably better to stay together, anyway.

Alexander was in the shallows, fishing something shape-less out of the water when she reemerged from the forest onto the bank.

"Huzzah!" he cried out. He dragged the sodden lump onto the shore. "I found one of our ration bags." Then he grasped his sword sheath sadly. "But Delphine . . . my sword. It's gone. It must have fallen out and been swept downstream."

As if she didn't feel guilty enough already. Delphine summoned her courage and looked him in the eye. "Alexander," she said, talking quickly to get it over with as fast as she could. "Maybe you're right. Maybe the needle is more dangerous than I care to admit. But it's the only clue I have to who I am, and it's also the reason that a band of rats wants me dead. So I need to figure out how it works.

"But . . . I'll only practice with it during the day. And I'll be sure not to destroy any more boats," she added as an afterthought.

He grinned. "It's a deal."

Delphine looked over his shoulder at the waterlogged ration bag. "And thank you for finding that," she said, trying to make amends. "I'm sorry you lost your sword."

He shrugged. "I'm just glad I didn't lose you."

Delphine waited for her internal voice to groan at his cheesiness, but for once it was silent. She gave an embarrassed little shrug. "I'm glad I didn't lose you, either." Then she coughed. "So, uh, shall we start walking down the river? We must be nearly at the mouth."

❇ ❇ ❇

As they traveled, threading their way along the bank of the river, Delphine spent most of the time trying to get her needle to do something—*anything*—just to prove to herself she could. All afternoon she tapped it on the trees they walked past, spun it in the air, poked it all around her, and generally waved it with abandon until Alexander refused to walk within two tail's-lengths of her reach.

"Not interested in getting skewered with your magic," he said. He skipped ahead a few more paces.

But it didn't matter how hard she tried; nothing she did caused more than a few silvery sparks to flicker into existence. Finally she shoved it back into the sheath. "I'll try again tonight," she said. "I can't focus while I'm walking."

"Sounds like a plan." Alexander took the opportunity to slow down and walk next to her again.

That night, as she built a campfire on the bank, Delphine examined the dry twigs. *What if . . . ?* She pulled her needle from the sheath, holding it carefully, remembering the silvery tingle that had leapt from the needle into her paws the night before. It had happened as she had looked up at the stars and the moon. She gazed toward the sky, and at the stars peeking through the clouds here and there. She let her gaze soften, slowing her breathing, then looked back down at the needle. If she could connect with that power without letting it take her over . . .

She pictured the silver sparks that had appeared earlier. As she imagined them leaping from the needle again, they became so real in her mind that she could nearly see them.

The needle trembled in her grasp, and a shower of sparks burst into existence, landing on the twigs. They were ablaze in an instant.

She gasped. "I did it! Alexander, did you see? I lit the fire!"

He turned around from where he had been hanging up

his waistcoat to air on a bramble. "Oh? Yes, nicely done. Good show."

Delphine rolled her eyes and turned back to the little fire, the needle still warm in her paws. She could do magic!

✳ ✳ ✳

Delphine smelled the ocean before she could see it. Her nose twitched with the unfamiliar smell as they hiked around one last bend in the river and then came face-to-face with the endless black sea. It had been almost two weeks since they had left the monastery, but they had finally made it. They could see the cliffs where Parfumoisson was supposed to lie according to Father Guillaume's map, but not one building or lighthouse gave a hint of civilization. The late-afternoon sun was already low in the sky.

Where were they supposed to go?

Delphine and Alexander walked out farther on the small stretch of beach until they had a clear view along the coastline. Now they could see the docks of a human town directly to the north. If they hurried, they could reach Parfumoisson before dinner.

The sun was falling quickly, broad bands of orange and red reflecting off the ocean and up onto the cliffs. As they walked, it seemed as if the beach was narrowing. Delphine stopped and looked back. No, it wasn't her imagination. The edge of the water was definitely getting closer to the base of the cliffs.

"Uh, Alexander?" Delphine stopped. "I think the ocean is, well, moving toward us." It sounded absurd. "Can it *do* that?"

Alexander glanced at the water, and his ears went white. "The tide," he said. "The ocean *is* coming toward us, and it's going to keep coming. Delphine, we need to go. We need to go now."

In an instant, Delphine realized what he was saying. Picking up her skirts, she began to run. They moved in tighter to the base of the cliff, hugging it as closely as they could, but the water was already lapping viciously at their paws. Delphine panted as she pushed herself to run even faster, the needle sheath bouncing against her back.

Only a sliver of sun remained, trembling above the horizon. A wave swept in around Delphine's legs and nearly knocked her over. She stumbled against the cliff rocks and felt the stones scrape her paws, but she managed to catch her balance. Another wave hit both of them hard, and they fell. Delphine pushed herself up again, tasting the salt water in her mouth. She looked back over her shoulder.

"Go!" Alexander cried.

Delphine glanced at the horizon just in time to see a faint green flash, and then the sun was gone. Another wave, the largest yet, picked her up and smashed her against the cliff.

"Alexander!" she screamed. And then she was pulled under.

Chapter 13

another wave crashed over Delphine, knocking the breath out of her. She clutched desperately to the cliff stones as the water buffeted her from every direction. When the wave finally receded, she could breathe again. She heard Alexander's claws scrabbling on the rock behind her.

The dock pillars beckoned ahead, the closest only a few tail's-lengths away. As soon as the next wave passed, Delphine shoved off the rocks as hard as she could, hoping Alexander was doing the same. She lashed her tail as she swam, the ocean water freezing cold. Then her paws bumped up against the wood of the pillar. She scrambled upward out of the waves.

Alexander was climbing up the other side of the post. They both reached the top and collapsed on the slats of the dock, gasping for breath. Finally, he lifted his head and looked at her.

"No more water," he said. "I don't care where we go next on this quest of yours. But no lakes, streams, oceans, or springs. I'm tired of nearly drowning."

When they had finally regained their strength, they looked up at where they had landed. The dock stretched toward a sheltered cove with a tiny beach, large enough for four or five human boats to be pulled up on the sand. Cliffs surrounded the town of Parfumoisson on the other three sides. A path climbed steeply upward from the tiny harbor through the town.

Now I'll find some answers, Delphine thought as they started up the road.

"Now I'll be able to get my doublet cleaned and my whiskers restyled properly," Alexander said out loud.

Delphine laughed despite herself.

The town was nestled into the curve of the cliffs behind the cove, houses stacked one on top of another so closely that they appeared to be hanging on to the craggy walls like barnacles. Narrow cobblestoned streets squeezed their way between the buildings. Delphine and Alexander spotted the welcome signs of animal inhabitants everywhere. A mouse-size door carved above a lintel. Tiny stairs curling up around a window box. A row of glass-paned windows, each no larger than a human thumbnail, just below the eaves of a human roof.

The sky had dropped into inky night and candles glowed in the windows of both human and animal dwellings, but the town seemed oddly silent. Every one of the shopfronts was shuttered and dark.

"Where are all the humans?" whispered Delphine.

"Let's just count our blessings that they're not out here, trying to capture us with their traps," said Alexander. "I think maybe it has something to do with the change of seasons. It's a fishing town, isn't it?" He pointed at the canvas-covered boats pulled up on the beach behind them. "Maybe they mainly stay inside this time of year."

That made some sense, although it raised another question in Delphine's mind. "So they don't fish for the entire winter? How do they get by?"

Alexander shrugged. "Perhaps they dry fish in the summer months, like how we preserve and put up vegetables?"

That wasn't something Delphine ever expected to hear from Alexander. "How do you know about putting up vegetables?"

He shrugged again. "I used to sneak down to the castle kitchens, remember?"

Delphine shook her head. "Alexander de Soucy Perrault, just when I think I've got you all figured out." A cat yowled somewhere in the distance, and they both jumped. "Come on. Let's find a safe place to spend the night."

They headed up the main street, Delphine keeping her eyes peeled for a mouse inn.

"Look!" Alexander pointed to a tiny stone plaque at the very base of a building, far below the human-size sign overhead. "The animals of this town have their own street names. 'Rue Moule.' And there's 'Rue Balthazar.'" He read off the little street signs as they walked. "'Rue Huître.' 'Rue Champignon.'"

The buildings were growing narrower and taller. Ornate carvings of sea creatures decorated the lintels and doorframes. Delphine caught sight of a cheese shop and then a vegetable stand, both with separate mouse entrances, both closed for the night.

"'Rue Bouillabaisse,'" Alexander reported next to her. They were coming into the center square, with a horse trough on the left and an impressive church on the right. "'Rue Fortencio.'"

"Alexander, maybe we should—" she began, then stopped. "Wait! Did you say *Fortencio?*"

He pointed to the old stone plaque affixed at the bottom of a nearby wall, with an arrow pointing down a side street. It read RUE FORTENCIO in carefully carved letters, just big enough for a mouse to see, but small enough to go unnoticed by humans.

"That's the surname of the music master!" Delphine dug in her apron pocket for the scrap of vellum. "It can't be a coincidence!" She headed down the side street, tail twitching excitedly, scanning the buildings carefully.

If they hadn't been looking for it, they would have missed it completely. Halfway down the block on the left side, at the base of a human church, decorative stone panels had been mounted long ago on either side of a pair of mouse-size stone doors. Looking at the panels up close, Delphine could make out music notes in the carvings. The stones seemed ancient, worn by centuries of summer sun and winter frosts. The hinges, the handles, even the intricate lock that overlapped both doors . . . everything was coated in a fine layer of peeling red rust. Delphine reached out to trace her paw along one of the music notes.

"This was Fortencio Académie," she breathed. "I'm sure of it. And that means my ancestor was here, too. The mouse with the needle and the silver whiskers. We have to get inside!"

"Now?" squeaked Alexander.

"Why not?"

"Well." He hesitated. "It might be—"

"Haunted?" She quirked an eyebrow.

"That is *not* what I was going to say," he insisted. "What if it's, well, dangerous? Structurally unsound? These old buildings can appear to be sturdy, yet interior-wise . . ."

Delphine pushed on one of the door handles, but it was closed tight. The lock had some sort of detailing, but she couldn't make it out under the years of rust. Brushing flakes off her paw, Delphine stepped back, staring at the doors thoughtfully. Then, in a moment of inspiration, she withdrew her needle. Alexander eyed her nervously but said nothing.

Letting her needle rest gently in her grasp, Delphine closed her eyes, feeling the softness of the silvery whispers beginning to tingle in her paws. That rust . . . there was solid metal somewhere beneath it. She pictured moonlight flowing over the lock, washing away the flakes of decay.

Alexander gasped and her eyes popped open. A gentle shimmer was streaming from the needle, blowing away the rust like dead leaves in a breeze.

They leaned forward, examining the now-shining metal lock. It was formed with a series of interlocking panels, each etched with a musical note. Delphine stared in frustration, and her momentary elation vanished. She might as well have been staring at a series of Greek symbols.

"*B, D, A, C-sharp, C, D, G,*" said Alexander nonchalantly.

"You can read music?"

He gave her an odd look. "Of course. Growing up in the castle, everyone has to learn how to play an instrument. It's item number four in Oddsley's *Traits of the Genteel Mouse.*"

She looked blankly at him. "Is that a book?"

"A handbook, actually." He hummed the music notes aloud.

The series of tones struck a chord in her. "Do that again."

He did, and she focused hard. It wasn't quite right, but if reshuffled, the notes made her think of bedtime, her mother's embrace, tucking the pinkie mice into their cribs. The memory made her heart soar. *Of course!* It was the oldest lullaby she knew.

Whiskers soft and eyes are closed, she sang softly. *Time for baby mine to doze.*

"Alexander! That's it!" She hummed the melody again, a little louder. "All the notes are there, just in the wrong order. We have to rearrange the order to match the song!"

"Sing that once more." He listened as she hummed. "*D* . . . *A* . . . *G* . . . *B* . . . *D* . . . *C-sharp* . . . *C*," he said slowly.

Delphine reached out and pressed the panels on the lock in order. *D, A, G, B, D, C#, C.*

There was a soft click. She pushed cautiously on one of the handles, and the door swung open noiselessly, despite the rust on the hinges. Delphine looked at Alexander. "Would you care to join me?"

He hesitated, then nodded and followed her across the threshold.

The hallway that stretched in front of them was wide and low, with empty sconces on both sides. Soot coated the ceiling overhead in dark streaks. Moonlight from the open doorway dappled the ancient flagstones beneath their paws.

"See? That wasn't so hard," she said jovially.

Alexander narrowed his eyes. "So now you're just going to wander around an abandoned music school in the middle of the night, with no light, until you find, what? A tapestry that tells the story of who your ancestor was, why she had that needle, what she did here, and all the other answers you're hoping to find?"

"That's the plan," she said, marching forward.

He sighed and fell in behind her. "Who knows what creatures might still be lurking down here?" he mused out loud.

"Centipedes love living underground, and they can be dangerous when provoked. Termites, ants . . ." He shuddered a little. "Do you hear something down the hall? Skittering feet? Thousands of tiny claws scratching over the stone?"

Delphine shot him a deadpan stare. "So that oath you took to protect me . . . I gather it doesn't apply to dark passages?"

She turned to continue onward, then stopped and pointed at an alcove in the wall. There was an age-darkened plaque with what appeared to be a shrine laid out below it. Burned-down candles, long-dried flower petals, ancient anise seeds. "Look!"

"I still hear skittering, and it's definitely getting louder," Alexander mumbled.

She peered at the plaque in the dim moonlight. "*'Cécile Montroulard, née 1661, morte 1682,'*" she read aloud, tracing her fingers across the lettering. "*'Soprano, Sword Master, Protector of Our School. Bravest is the one who sacrifices all.'* How sad. I wonder what happened?"

But the answer was lost to time. They left the shrine behind, heading down the hallway, which grew darker with every step. Delphine started to think it might have been prudent to wait until morning after all, but she'd be bee-stung if she was going to admit to Alexander that he had been right.

Scrrrritchhhh.

Delphine's whiskers twitched nervously. "Alexander," she whispered. "Do you hear that? That scratching sound?"

"That's what I've been saying," he whispered back, his voice strained.

It was a scrabbly, scuttering noise. She pressed herself against the nearest wall. It seemed to be getting closer. Which direction was it coming from?

Then another sound joined the mix. Voices. Many voices, rising in deep, ominous harmony.

Delphine and Alexander clung together, shuddering.

"What is that?" Alexander finally managed to whisper.

"Singing, I think." Delphine listened, trying to calm her beating heart. "You were right. Someone's down here."

They listened for another minute. The singing didn't seem to be getting any closer, but it wasn't fading away, either. The low, eerie tones echoed down the pitch-black hallways. It made her fur stand on end, but she couldn't stop listening. The longer they stood, the more it drew her in.

On a sudden impulse, she turned back to Alexander. "We need to go find the source of it."

"Why—?" He stopped himself and sighed. "If you say so."

With Delphine leading the way, they continued to feel along the stone wall through the inky blackness.

A thought struck Delphine. She held up her needle and pictured the silvery rays of the moon, holding the image in her mind as clearly as she could. The needle grew warm, and then it began to glow faintly. *There.* The passageway was still dark, but the needle gave off enough of the pale silver light to make the flagstones visible beneath their paws.

They tiptoed closer and closer toward the sounds until they could see the outline of a door recessed in the stone wall. Delphine rested her paw on the dusty metal handle. The scratching sound and ominous voices were definitely coming from the other side of the wall. With a deep breath, Delphine pushed the handle and the door slowly scraped inward, hinges squeaking in protest.

The light on the other side of the door was so bright that they were momentarily blinded. As they blinked, they began to make out a large round stone room, with a vaulted ceiling far at the top. Stubs of candles ringed the edges. In the center a swarm of hooded figures stood in concentric circles around a curious device, singing the strange harmony they had heard. Now she could hear the lyrics as well.

Ever onward comes the night, leading toward tomorrow's day.
And the moon who brings us light, waxes full, then fades away.
Passing through the seasons fair, then the seasons dark and cold.
Till the cycle starts again, year by year the story's told.

Delphine and Alexander stood unnoticed, taking in the scene. At the center of the singers was a hunched figure, whiskers springing out from either side of its hood. The figure was turning a crank that rotated a series of gears leading upward. Delphine's gaze moved up to where the gears touched the domed ceiling. She gasped.

She had been so intent on the hooded singers that she had

missed the magnificent painting above—a scene that circled upon itself without end. It showed towns, mountains, pastures, streams: a whole countryside. As her eye traveled over the mural, Delphine saw the changing of the seasons—trees springing to life, then heavy with fruit, followed by red leaves fluttering until snow lay thick on the branches and the whole cycle began again. A long series of tiny numbers wrapped around the bottom. She noticed an intricately carved arm of metal pointing to one of the numbers just below the autumn scene.

Delphine's jaw dropped. "It's a calendar," she breathed. The metal arm was being cranked from one date to the next, its point dragging on the stone. It was the scratching sound they had heard.

The figures sang on, still unaware of the two mice who had tiptoed into their midst.

Delphine turned to whisper to Alexander, but he was no longer by her side. He had stepped forward out of the shadows, paws akimbo on his hips. "Demons of the underground, you shall not harm us!" he cried with fervor.

The figures turned, the song silenced on their lips. The skittering of the crank ceased. The air hung still, just for a moment.

"What are you doing?" squeaked Delphine in horror.

But Alexander was already charging toward the hooded figures.

KING MIDNIGHT'S BODY ACHED, A deep, dull pain that reached all the way to his bones.

He was cold, so cold. He inched his chair closer to the fire, but the heat had no effect. He could feel his blood running sluggishly through his veins. His scars throbbed.

He hadn't experienced the sensation of pain in a very long time. And there was something else, too, something he had never expected to feel. He was feeling *old*. Was the magic beginning to weaken after all this time? He had stayed by the source faithfully, no matter where his troops ventured. Could the power be fading? He thrust the thought away from him, turning back to the mouse skulls arranged on his mantelpiece.

Midnight's paws were numb. He rubbed them together violently, then pulled his cape tight around his shoulders. The faded black velvet, still buttery soft, draped over his bony figure.

"My king." One of his guards had entered. "News from Snurleau. He's sent a messenger." She bowed and withdrew, letting the envoy into the throne room.

In came a country rat with dull, matted fur and a straw cap in his paws. He bowed low. "Pleased to meet you, my king," he said excitedly. "Never thought I'd actually be called up for service."

King Midnight waved his paw petulantly. "You're just delivering a message. At least you were able to follow Snurleau's directions to get here. I trust he paid you enough?"

The rat nodded. "He did say I'd get the rest of my reward once I arrived."

Ah, yes. Ever-cunning Snurleau. King Midnight motioned again. "The message?"

"Snurleau reports the following." The rat took a breath and recited carefully. "He's found the needle. The two mice are heading west along the river. He's tracking them, but he needs more help before he can engage." He twisted his cap in his paws. "Not sure what that all means, Your Majesty, but I memorized it word for word, just as Snurleau said it."

Midnight's eyes were aflame. He rose from his chair by the fireplace, cape swirling around him. Perhaps it was his imagination, but the pain in his joints seemed to have lessened. "Mezzo!" he roared.

The rat guard marched back into the throne room. "My king?"

"Send for Valentine!" He glanced back at the sniveling rat who had brought the message. "And this one is to get his *reward.*"

Mezzo's face fell.

King Midnight sighed. Overall, Mezzo was the best head guard he'd ever had, but sometimes he wished she were a little more blood-thirsty.

Luckily, he had plenty of other guards to help on that front. "Woefull!" he bellowed. Another guard marched in smartly with a wicked grin, having overheard the conversation thus far. "Take this rat." Woefull winked at King Midnight and dragged the rat away. Now that this country rat knew where the fortress was located, he could either live there to serve Midnight, or not live at all.

A few minutes later, Mezzo returned, Valentine following close behind. The snow-white ermine oozed her way into the crown room, wrapping herself around one of the worn-out armchairs and settling into it without invitation. Her dark eyes sparkled with curiosity.

King Midnight smiled, lips curling back. He had few trustworthy minions outside of his rats, but Valentine was one of his best. "My dear Valentine," he began, rubbing his paws together, "I have a most exciting mission for you. Snurleau is already in the field. You must find him and help him take down the two mice he's trailing."

Valentine didn't blink. "You mean the two mice with the needle."

How did she know that? Under different circumstances, he might have been afraid of her. But she had proved her loyalty many times over. "Yes," he replied, feigning nonchalance. "Find them and bring me that needle. Dispose of the mice as you see fit."

The ermine stretched langorously, then rose up out of the chair. She cracked her knuckles and swished her tail. "Consider it done." In a silent flash of white, she was gone.

The room lay still for a moment. Then Mezzo cleared her throat. "What if Snurleau's already lost them?"

"Silence!" roared King Midnight.

Mezzo bowed and withdrew to her post outside the great doors.

He turned back to the row of skulls. *Soon I will unlock your secrets*, he thought.

But the skulls stared back at him, saying no more than they had for the last hundred years.

Chapter 14

alexander lunged straight toward the circle of mysterious hooded figures. "Always be on the offense!" he cried over his shoulder at Delphine as he ran.

She gritted her teeth and headed after him.

The figure at the crank straightened, whiskers twitching once. Then both paws shot out toward Alexander. "Stop!" came an imperious alto voice. The figure pulled back her hood to reveal the visage of a sharp-looking shrew. She was definitely not happy to see them, but she was also, it appeared, not a mouse-eating monster.

Delphine poked Alexander hard in the side. "Nice job making a good first impression," she hissed.

The shrew stood tall and commanding, black eyes snapping. "You are trespassing on the grounds of the Fortencio Académie. I bid you, introduce and explain yourselves."

Delphine squeaked in surprise. The school still existed?

Alexander eyed the attentive chorus of onlookers. "We thought you were ghosts . . . or worse. But you're clearly not." He coughed awkwardly. Then he bowed low. "Lord Alexander de Soucy Perrault, of the Poirier Perraults, at your service."

Delphine curtsied alongside him. "Delphine Desjardins." She snuck a peek at the rest of the figures. Were these, then, current students of the school?

"Welcome," said the shrew, but her voice was cold. "I fear you have come at an inopportune time." She glanced behind them at the half-open door. "And in a most inopportune manner."

Delphine now saw that the door she and Alexander had come through lay hidden behind a dusty tapestry and had clearly been unused for at least a hundred years, if not more.

"May we assist you in finding your way out," continued the shrew. It was very clear that this was not a question. "You have arrived during our nightly intonation, when we rotate our calendar to the next date. And we have not yet completed our task." The other figures pulled back their hoods to reveal the rest of the singers. Most of the students were shrews, though there were a few mice and hedgehogs. Several, including a squirrel in the back row, stared darkly at them.

Delphine realized that if they escorted her out now, she might never get a chance to ask for help in their quest. She curtseyed again, this time even deeper. "I apologize for the unintentional intrusion," she began quickly. "We come only seeking knowledge. We have traveled long and wish to learn if you have any information that could help solve a great mystery."

The shrew eyed her but said nothing. Encouraged, Delphine continued: "There was a mouse, a hundred years ago, who might have come here for shelter. A mouse with silver whiskers, chased by rats that wanted to kill her. She had something of theirs—a needle." She paused. How safe was it to reveal more? Deciding she had to take the risk, Delphine reached up behind her and pulled her needle out of its sheath.

Most of the students took a step back, but the head shrew did not. She looked at the needle curiously. "Come back in the morning," she said. "We shall speak then." She turned and scanned her students. "Melchior, escort these two to the door. The *front* door," she added, for Delphine and Alexander's benefit. Then she turned her back on them and gestured to her students. "Let us continue," she said firmly. As the shrew cranked the lever again, the voices lifted once more in their strange song.

The squirrel Melchior glared at them from an archway on the other side of the vault, his oversize tail flipping in an irritated fashion. "Come," he said curtly, clearly displeased at having to leave the ceremony. He led them through a tangle of dark halls and out to the front of the building.

He shoved open the massive gates outside the main doors. The two mice passed through, and then Delphine paused. "Do you know where we can stay for the night?"

"No idea," said the squirrel, slamming the gates with a resounding bang and disappearing back inside.

"Cad!" cried Alexander, jostling the metal angrily. The loud clanging reverberated off the cobblestones.

Delphine looked around. It seemed as if they had exited on the other side of the human church. "We'll come back tomorrow. Let's go find a safe place to sleep."

Alexander was now biting his thumb at the gates as if Melchior could still see him. "The nerve of that squirrel! To throw us out after we've come so far!"

Delphine grabbed his arm and began to drag him away. There were more important things than arguing with a locked gate in the middle of a cold, dark street. "Come on. We still have to find somewhere to sleep."

They headed back down toward the main town square, eyes peeled for a safe nook or cranny. Then Delphine noticed a sudden movement just a few steps down the street. A group of shadowy figures, emerging from a hole in the wall.

Rats.

"Hide!" she whispered to Alexander. They ducked behind a pile of pebbles. The rats' voices echoed clearly in the still night air.

". . . not just a rumor," one of the rats was saying with emphasis. "They're after two mice, they are."

"Who is, then?" came another voice.

Delphine tried to peer around the pebbles but was yanked back by Alexander.

"All of the king's troops, they are," was the reply. "And set to kill 'em, too, for a needle."

A high-pitched laugh came sharply through the night air. "A needle! Well, I never!"

"True, though I heard . . ."

The voices faded as the rats meandered down the street. When all was silent again, Delphine and Alexander emerged, brushing off pebble dust.

"We can't stay here," observed Alexander.

"We *have* to stay here," Delphine retorted. "But just until we find out what we need to know. All right?"

Alexander sighed. "Let's just find somewhere to sleep."

✳ ✳ ✳

Somewhere to sleep turned out to be a cozy hole in the wall of a human bakery, nestled between two bricks of the oven's outer side. Best of all, the bricks were still warm from the day's baking. They wedged a dead leaf across the entrance to block themselves from view, then each snuggled into a corner of the little space and dozed off.

Several hours later, human voices from inside the building woke Delphine. It seemed the baker and her apprentices had arrived. In the darkness Delphine could see Alexander sitting in the crack between the stones. He appeared to be staring out at the empty street.

"Alexander?"

"The humans woke me up," he whispered back. "So I thought I'd keep watch for a while. Go back to sleep."

She lay quietly, listening to the soft sounds of dough being kneaded and wood crackling in the oven. It made her think of Maman in their kitchen, paws covered in flour as she rolled out a pie crust. Delphine had always complained about having turnip pie for dinner, but right now she would have given anything for just one bite.

The humans chattered gaily as they worked.

". . . searching all across the kingdom, but nobody knows who she is," one was saying.

Delphine's ears perked up in surprise for the second time that evening. How could the humans possibly know about her search for her ancestor?

But then the voice continued, "All she left behind was a glass slipper. That poor prince—found his love and lost her in a single night."

So they were talking about the human ball. She sighed. It seemed so long ago now. Delphine snuggled in tighter, wondering if Cinderella had been able to finish the gowns and attend after all. Had Cinderella seen the mystery princess?

Another voice came, high and crackly. "Who makes shoes out of glass, anyway? Sounds like typical royal foolishness to me." All the voices laughed in agreement.

"Well, if you ask me, the prince should . . ." started the first voice.

But Delphine never heard what the prince should do. She had fallen back asleep.

Chapter 15

Someone was calling for Delphine, loudly.

She had to wake up, she had to run. The rats were coming and they would kill her if they found her. The needle. Where was her needle? She could no longer feel it in her paws.

"Delfie!" came the voice again from a long way off.

She struggled to blink open her eyes. She felt as if she were climbing through a thick fog of sleep. The rats. Were they coming?

"Delfie!" The voice seemed closer now.

Delphine awoke in their makeshift nest in the bakery wall. Her ears were sweaty where they were pressed against the hot brick, but her rear paws were hanging out into the chilly open air of the outdoors. Someone grabbed her tail unceremoniously.

"Ow!" she yelped as she leapt up, hitting her head on the corner of a brick. The resulting cascade of mortar dust sent her into a sneezing fit.

There came another yank on her tail. "Delfie! Wake up!"

She launched herself from the nest with all four paws outspread in attack, landing fully on the instigator below.

Too late, Delphine registered the familiar doublet and ruddy-colored fur. As she collided with Alexander, a good-size crumb of bread flew out of his paw and landed in a nearby pool of slimy-looking water.

He leapt up immediately, brushing off the combination of flour and dirt from his doublet. "Allow me to help you," he said, proffering his paw.

Delphine lay there flat on her back, staring up at the early-morning sky. She had just attacked him as a thank-you for bringing her a delicious-looking crumb. Maybe it was time to stop leaping to conclusions.

"My lady?" His worried face came into view. "Are you hurt?"

"No, no," she responded. This brought on another fit of sneezing. "And please stop saying 'my lady.'" Then another thought occurred to her. "Did you call me 'Delfie' a moment ago?"

He blushed. "My apologies. I thought you might enjoy some breakfast."

"I saw the crumb," she replied sheepishly. "That was very kind of you. I'm sorry that I—"

At her words, Alexander perked up so quickly that his ears popped with happiness. "I shall gather another!" He dashed back into the side door of the bakery, returning a few moments later completely covered in flour with an even larger crumb, this one taking both paws to carry.

Delphine smiled, thanking him. They walked slowly toward the church, munching on the fresh bread and its crackling crust as they went.

At the entrance to the music school, Delphine paused. The head shrew hadn't given them her name. And, Delphine realized, neither she nor Alexander had thought to ask for it. She glanced at Alexander as she knocked on the gates, and found he had managed to brush away all the flour. In fact, he looked as if he had just gotten his whiskers freshly curled and his cloak reflounced. How *did* he do that?

A little serving-shrew met them at the gates. "Wait here, if you please," he said, bringing them into the entryway.

"Thank you," said Delphine. "We're here to see—"

But the serving-shrew had already scurried into the depth of the halls and disappeared around a corner.

Delphine looked around curiously. Dark wood panels formed doors that separated the main spaces into smaller, less drafty rooms. Yet it was clear the whole school had been constructed within the stone passages laid down hundreds of years earlier, probably when the human church was originally built. Now that Delphine knew they were underneath the floor of the human church, the low but wide stone ceilings made more sense.

Only a few windows pierced the front rooms. The sconces they had seen in the abandoned passages the night before had been built into these walls as well, but smaller and higher, as if their design had become more refined over time. The stones beneath their paws were covered in a series of long, woven runners, cream with touches of embroidery. She realized they were made of discarded human robes, the usable portions separated into carpet-like runners. *How clever!*

Peering beyond the entryway, Delphine noticed polished rounds of metal placed at regular intervals down the corridor, almost like a series of the mirrors that Princess Petits-Oiseaux had in her dressing suite. Though as Delphine peered into them, the mouse looking back at her was wavy and blurred. *Not very effective*, she thought.

Then the strains of an unfamiliar song trickled from a nearby open door. The voices were soft and sweet, but the words struck a chord deep within Delphine. She listened raptly.

Ere the night has turned to morn,
True the paw that pulls the thread,

Tho' the light of day is born,
Full the silver in its stead.

Delphine took a stealthy step closer to the door, hoping to make out the lyrics more clearly. Alexander shot her a glance, but she ignored him, focusing on the words.

Once a pattern comes to be,
None but blood who wove it fair,
Can undo the magic lee,
Can unweave with time to spare.

Her attention was interrupted by the sound of pawfalls. The little serving-shrew reappeared before she could step away from the open door. He gave her a sharp glance and pulled the door shut as he passed. Chastened, she returned to stand next to Alexander.

"I tried to warn you," Alexander whispered as the serving-shrew took their traveling cloaks and bustled away through another door. "I can already tell. They're very particular."

A moment later, the music master from the previous night appeared and bowed low. "Rolanta Fortencio, master of the Fortencio School of Music." Her voice was a deep alto, unusual for a shrew. She clasped their paws, each in turn. "I hope we are meeting on better terms today. Please, come." Turning, she strode down the hall at a rapid pace.

Delphine and Alexander trotted after her. They made several quick turns around interlinked doorways and ended in a jewelry box of a sitting room, with rows of bookshelves and a puffed-velvet ceiling.

"What a lovely room," Alexander gushed. "You have made it your very own."

Rolanta Fortencio gestured at a pair of velvet armchairs that seemed to have been constructed from a human purse, the pearl trim now edging the seat of each chair. "Will you both sit?"

"Madame Fortencio," Delphine said as sweetly as she could once they were settled in the overstuffed chairs, "I cannot thank you enough for your generosity in helping with my endeavor."

The music master smiled briskly. "I am most happy to assist. What were you hoping to find?"

"The mouse with the needle. And the silver whiskers."

"Yes . . . the story of the mouse's visit is part of school lore. It is particularly curious that you found your way through the back passages, since that was the main entrance to the school at the time of that mouse's visit." Fortencio stroked her whiskers thoughtfully. "Likely a mere coincidence, but still fascinating. One hundred years ago, a mouse with silver whiskers sought shelter here, bearing a strangely emblazoned needle of immense proportions." She paused, giving Delphine a sharp glance. "One hundred years later, another mouse has appeared with the same silver whiskers, also bearing an oversize needle, now asking after the first mouse." She fell quiet, musing.

Delphine's tail started to twitch, thinking of Father Guillaume's similar observation. She hooked her paw around her tail to keep it still. "Do you know who the mouse was?" she prompted as lightly as she could when she could bear the silence no more.

Rolanta Fortencio looked up at her. "Know who she was? Oh no, no. I know nothing more than the tidbit of school history I just related. But I am certain it all exists in the school's archives."

Archives! Now they were getting somewhere. Delphine's mind flashed to the meticulously organized Tymbale records on the endless shelves, alphabetized and reaching back hundreds of years. "Can you take us there?"

Rolanta seemed suddenly ill at ease. "They are . . . not easy to access."

"Please. I've traveled so far." She paused. "I'll be extremely careful with your papers. Whatever you need, however they're stored, I will respect your rules. But it's truly a matter of life or death that I find more information about that mouse."

The music master's mouth pursed. "I will take you to where they are stored. But I warn you, you may not wish to stay for too long. That part of the school lies within the area you traversed last night. It can be . . ." She looked around the room as if hoping that the word she was casting for might be written on the spine of a book. Finding no such assistance, she was forced to finally look back at them. ". . . off-putting," she finished, rising.

But Delphine was already picturing rows of ordered archive ledgers. She practically floated out of the room and down the hall.

As the music master led them along the passageway, she paused by the entrance to the school kitchens. "One moment, please." A mouthwatering smell wafted out. She ducked in and returned with a napkin full of fresh cookies that she proffered to the two mice. "A quick midmorning snack."

Delphine bit into one. It was warm and buttery, redolent of a flavorful spice. "Is that . . . anise seed?" she asked in delight.

"It is," the music master replied, smiling. "These cookies are a specialty of the Fortencio Académie kitchens. They're prepared every morning—a tradition that goes back before anyone can remember." She continued down the corridor, the two mice following behind.

True to Rolanta's word, they continued to walk for longer than Delphine thought possible. It was a warren of corridors and tunnels, winding farther and farther beneath the church. The air was growing close and musty, a sure sign that these passages were rarely used.

"Don't you come back here regularly to update the records?" Delphine asked hesitantly, ducking under another swath of cobwebs.

"The newer archives are now held in the front area of the school," Rolanta responded shortly.

At least there was plenty of light, Delphine observed, even this deep into the corridors. The sheets of metal she had dismissed as vanity mirrors were in fact no such thing. They reflected a thin stream of daylight from one to the next, cantilevering the light down halls and around corners. It was enough to make a candle unnecessary, even this far from a window. Delphine marveled at such a cunning design.

"Was this all created by the same animals who made the moving calendar we saw last night?" Delphine asked, examining one of the metal discs with new appreciation as they passed.

"It was indeed," confirmed Rolanta. "This school was founded by some of the most brilliant minds of their time."

Delphine noticed a narrow archway on their left that led into an empty, crumbling passageway. She paused, peering inside.

"Is that . . . ?"

"The old hallways you were wandering around in last night? Yes." Rolanta's voice was tight, warning against further questions, but Delphine continued unheeded.

"Didn't you say that this part of the school was in use when the mouse visited here? Can we go in there again and look around? If nothing's been touched since then, maybe there are clues." Delphine was still standing in the archway, nose twitching.

Rolanta Fortencio cleared her throat. "That area has been off-limits for a century due to structural disrepair. If you would be so kind as to follow me . . ."

Delphine realized that Alexander was swiftly shaking his

head, warning her not to push any further. She blushed and dropped back in behind Rolanta. "Of course."

The music master continued down several more hallways. Finally she turned a corner and Delphine noticed a little shudder creep across her face. "Here we are."

They had stopped in front of a low, arched door with an ugly metal handle, sharp like a branch of thorns. The light in the tunnel had grown dim. "Welcome to the archives." She stepped backward and gestured at the handle. She seemed unwilling to touch it herself.

The heavy door swung open slowly beneath Delphine's paw, and she stepped into a triangular foyer. The air was so thick and still that it pressed heavy on her chest. Corridors stretched away in either direction, filled with teetering, worm-eaten stacks of papers. Folios lay bent and broken everywhere she looked, their pages spilling into bins and boxes that were, in turn, sagging under the weight of endless ledgers. After the organized files of Tymbale, it was a painful sight.

"Take as long as you like," the shrew said. She was still standing in the doorway, apparently unwilling to step farther inside. Delphine noticed that her ears had gone pale. "I must go. I shall send someone to collect you when dinner is served."

"Thank you," said Delphine, baffled by the shrew's nervousness.

Rolanta turned. "Pay no mind to any odd occurrences," she called over her shoulder as she disappeared back down the hall.

Delphine looked at Alexander.

"Well, she's a curious character," he said, cocking an eyebrow.

"Almost as if she were scared to stay," she responded. "What is she afraid of, a pile of ledgers falling on her?"

Alexander shrugged. "At least there's plenty of information in here."

But Delphine had already stepped back into the hallway.

"Delfie? Where are you going?"

"The old area of the school. You really think we'll be able to find anything in those random piles of papers? I wouldn't even know where to start." She shook her head. "I'm going back to where we were last night."

"But . . . why?" Alexander looked positively befuddled.

"I just have a feeling," Delphine replied. She didn't know how to explain it, but something was pulling her back to those old hallways.

✳   ✳   ✳

The ancient stones were smooth under Delphine's paws. As she continued down the passageway, Alexander tiptoeing behind her, she could smell the air growing less stale. There was an inexplicable cool breeze wafting by.

Then the fur on the back of Delphine's neck stood up. She could feel someone watching her.

A dry, dusty voice came prickling out of the depths of the

hallway. *"What do you seek?"* The voice was high and sweet, but desiccated as ancient vellum.

"Who's there?" Delphine demanded, peering down the dim hall.

There was no answer.

Bits of daylight flickered and fluttered ahead, and Delphine's nostrils filled with the smell of . . . was that anise seed? The flavor of the cookies from the school's kitchen suddenly filled her mouth. She glanced at Alexander. He had backed up against the nearest wall, eyes wide.

"Did you hear that?" she whispered.

"Of course!" he replied, whiskers quivering.

The voice came again, now closer. *"What do you seek?"*

"I . . ." Delphine gulped, wheeling around to try to find who was speaking. "I need to learn about a mouse who came here long ago. She brought a needle—a needle like this one." She pointed to the sheath on her back. "But the music master, Speranta, sent her away to Tymbale Monastery." She waited, listening hard to the still air.

A long silence, and then: *"I know."* The voice made Delphine think of the sound of fabric slithering over dry wood.

"How do you know? What can you tell me?"

There was a soft sigh, and Delphine suddenly felt ice-cold. She shivered. The smell of anise came again, sweet and pungent.

Then a pillar of light began to form, beaming so brightly that it nearly blinded them. Delphine watched, transfixed, as the beam slowly coalesced into the figure of a mouse made of light. She was garbed in the armor of days long past, with a sword at her side, and her eyes were filled with a terrible sadness.

Delphine cried out and stumbled backward, paws flailing. She slammed into Alexander and they both fell to the ground.

When she looked up, the mouse was gone. The bright light had dissipated, replaced by normal daylight. The air was no longer cold, but she could still smell anise.

Alexander leapt upright. "A silly prank," he announced loudly. "One of the students, having fun at our expense."

But Delphine wasn't so sure.

A faint humming broke the silence. It seemed to be coming from behind her. She twisted this way and that, trying to find it, but the humming spun with her. She hesitated, then reached back to rest her paw on her needle. It was warm to the touch. When she pulled it out, the humming intensified.

What's happening? Delphine thought, panicked. The needle's vibrations ceased suddenly. The humming hiccupped and halted.

She paused. If the humming was part of the magic . . . She took a deep breath and let all worries drift from her mind, trusting in the needle. Sure enough, the vibration and the humming resumed.

"Delphine?" Alexander came closer. "You're starting to worry me."

"It's the needle," she responded. "It's trying to tell me

something." Now it sounded as though the humming was moving away from her. She followed it, needle still vibrating gently, the metal warm in her paws. Alexander trailed her as the humming led them down a corridor into an area that seemed familiar. Delphine tiptoed along, then noticed something ahead. That same shrine they had passed near the old entrance the night before. The humming came to a stop.

Delphine read the plaque again, more slowly, gnawing over each word. *Cécile Montroulard. Sword Master. Protecter of Our School.* She rubbed her paw against her cheek. Suddenly the air felt clammy. "Cécile," she said out loud, on a whim.

The humming shuddered through her bones, and cold air enveloped her from ears to toes.

Alexander squeaked. "What did you just do?"

"I didn't do anything!" Delphine nearly dropped her needle, but she managed to keep her grasp tight. "Ce-Cécile?" she stuttered. Surely ghosts didn't exist. She felt like a child, but she carried on. Whatever was happening, she was going to get to the bottom of it. And after magical needles, singing stars, and bloodthirsty rats, was a mouse ghost really so hard to believe?

Delphine twisted her paws even tighter around her needle. "Cécile," she said as firmly as she could, "if you're there, I beg you to help me."

Nothing.

Alexander shivered, watching intently.

Delphine tried again, despite her chattering teeth. "Please,

Cécile. I want to know why I'm here. Who I am. And . . ." Delphine was struck by a realization. Maybe she wasn't the only one who wanted to be known. ". . . I want to know who *you* are, too."

A warm breeze washed over her like the first day of spring. The fragrance of anise seeds sprang up again. Then light began to coalesce into the same figure of a mouse in the armor of a hundred years ago.

Cécile. Her eyes burning bright, she gazed at Delphine.

"Who are you?" Delphine breathed.

"Let me show you," Cécile said, her voice like wind whispering through the leaves. She came closer and the light swirled around Delphine, lifting her fur and blowing through her whiskers. A blast of pure white blinded her for a moment.

Delphine blinked. When she opened her eyes again, she was in the same hallway, but the floor was swept clean and the cobwebs were gone. Alexander was nowhere to be seen. Bright moonlight streamed through the doors in front of her, now open to the outside. She looked down to discover that she was wearing Cécile's armor.

She could hear the sounds of a battle in the street in front of her. A high scream, a mouse in pain. Without thinking, she ran forward and through the doors to see an army of rats forcing their way into the schoolyard. A battalion of mice and shrews were trying desperately to hold them at bay. And there, on the steps of the music school . . . there stood the silver-whiskered mouse.

Valentine sniffed the air. She could smell old wood, a chicken coop somewhere in the distance, a loaf of bread being baked . . . but still no Snurleau. She gnashed her teeth. Where in nutmegs was that nasty little stoat? She should have been able to smell his stench a thousand tail's-lengths away. She'd had to live with his odor stinking up the air at the fortress for far too long. But now that she actually *needed* to find that smell, it was nowhere.

Valentine wormed her way back into the blanket roll on the horse's back, where it was warm. The human and his horse were making good time. She would stay with them as long as she could get a free ride.

When the rider stopped for the night, she slithered out of the blanket roll and into the animal side of the tavern for a quick bite to eat. She knew this crossroads well, unfortunately. The animal tavern owner was a foul-mouthed toad who overcharged for watery mead and raised flies in the backyard. The odor of the fly farm was so vile that normally Valentine avoided this entire area like the plague. But it was also a stopping place for ne'er-do-wells of all types . . . just what Valentine needed right now. She would ask around quietly, see if Snurleau's name popped up in conversation, lay down some bread-crumbs.

The tavern door swung open and a wave of garlic and heat hit her square in the whiskers. The din was so loud that it seemed as if the entire county was visiting. She shouldered her way inside, past a horde of musky old rats and a few evil-looking shrews.

The crowd was singing along raucously as a lithe figure, prancing on the table, led them all with vigorous waves of his arms and nods of his head. The figure turned as he pranced, and Valentine got a noseful of his smell. Snurleau. *Finally.* No wonder she hadn't been able to smell him until now, with the fly-farm stench so thick.

"Ow! Ow! Lay off my ear!" Snurleau whined as Valentine dragged him through the tavern toward the side door. The crowd kept on singing, unperturbed at losing their ringleader. She spied the squat figure of Grenouille, the tavern owner, at the same time that he spotted her.

"Valentine!" He bowed his broad head to her, then opened his toady eyes wide. "We've not seen you for far too long." The tip of his fat tongue poked out through his lips as he spoke.

"The king keeps me busy," she said shortly.

"Ah yes . . . the king." The toad winked one bulbous eye at her.

Valentine pointed with her free paw toward the side door, her other paw still firmly clamped on Snurleau's ear. "Grenouille, would you mind if we stepped outside for a quiet conversation? Don't let other guests out that door for a few minutes, yes?"

He bowed obsequiously, his dirty apron strings dragging on the ground. She kicked open the door, shoved Snurleau through, then slammed it behind her. The stoat landed in a mud puddle and glared at Valentine.

"How dare you!" he spat. He rubbed at the mud on his breeches, but they were already so filthy that the mud was an improvement, if anything.

A long-abandoned human boot lay nearby in the yard. Valentine seated herself atop it like a throne. "King Midnight thinks you're tracking the mice," she commented. She twitched her tail lazily.

Snurleau grimaced. "Ah . . . yes. That's why you're here."

She went on. "You lost them, didn't you." This was a statement, not a question.

He grimaced again. "They got their paws on a boat and headed down the river. And I really, really hate the water."

Valentine yawned. "More than revenge?"

He stared at her, slack-jawed. "How do you know about . . . ?"

"You're going to catch one of Grenouille's flies like that."

He clamped his mouth shut. Then he opened it again. "Anyway, there were no other boats that I could afford with the little gold I had left. That's why I sent for reinforcements, see."

"So you came here to drown your sorrows, rather than heading down the river to try to catch up with them."

"We-e-e-lll . . ."

Valentine started cleaning her left paw. "Look. I don't really care why you let them get away. We'll head toward the river and then start tracking from there. With me in your corner, I'd say you'll have vengeance on that ruddy noblemouse in no time."

Snurleau nodded, his sly smile creeping back onto his face.

Chapter 16

Through the eyes of Cécile, a hundred years past, Delphine stared at the silver-whiskered mouse standing at the old entrance of the music school. The mouse clutched a bundle in one paw and the needle in the other, and the look on her face was of pure terror.

An elegant, dark-eyed shrew in long robes stood next to her. It could only be Speranta, the music master of the time. She pushed the mouse back inside the school. "Stay out of sight!"

But the mouse shoved forward again, her huge eyes fixed on the rats fighting their way through the gates. "They're here for me!" she cried. "I brought them to your doorstep. Let me draw them away."

"You're not risking death just to save us," retorted Speranta in anger. "They dare to threaten you? Then they threaten all of us. We are not defenseless." She gestured, and Delphine-as-Cécile found herself stepping forward. "Cécile is the finest swordsmouse south of the river. She'll distract them while you escape. Nobody need die today."

Cécile knelt before the silver-whiskered mouse. "The rats are enemies to us all. Run now, while you still can. Keep your baby safe."

Baby? The word crashed over Delphine.

Speranta turned to another of the shrews. "Take her to the tunnels. Show her the one that leads to the top of the cliffs." Then she spoke very quietly to the mouse. "Go upstream. Find Tymbale Monastery. Use my name; I am known there."

With thanks on her lips, the mouse fled, carrying the needle and her bundle—her *baby*—into the dark.

Cécile turned and faced the rats, drawing her mighty sword.

She fought more valiantly than Delphine could have ever imagined possible. Cécile was a dervish of swordplay, seeming to be in multiple places at once. She parried, riposted, and tore through row after row of marauding rats. From inside the school windows, the other students assisted as they could, using slingshots to harry the rats and keep them distracted.

But Cécile was growing weak. Delphine could feel the fatigue in her limbs, the struggle to keep lifting the sword. And Speranta must have seen it, too, because she stepped forward, head held high, and stood alongside Cécile. She faced the rats.

"I will tell you where the mouse has gone," Speranta announced. "But you must promise to leave and never return."

The rats sneered, their yellow fangs dripping with blood and spittle. "Why would we believe you?" said one.

"You have no choice," said Speranta bravely. "I alone know where she is. Either you hear my words, or I will disappear as well and the trail will be as cold and dead as your fallen comrades."

"Then tell us," demanded the same rat. He came closer and closer until Delphine could smell the stench of rotting meat on his breath.

"Arc des Dieux," said Speranta. "Up the river. She said something about a château."

The rats looked at one another. "But . . ." said one. Another scratched at her ear with a filthy paw, pondering. The lead rat's eyes widened.

"That cowardly mouse!" he screamed, whirling on the rest of his lot. "She's doubling back! She's heading back to Château Trois Arbres!" Their faces grew wide with understanding as well, then anger washed over their features. Speranta took another step toward the rats.

"Now go," she demanded. "I've told you what you came here to learn."

But the lead rat raised his great fist sheathed in a metal gauntlet, high over her head. "Maybe I'll take care of you first," he roared. Speranta fell back.

Like a fierce angel, Cécile came flying upon the rat, sword flashing through the air. With a single sweep of the blade she took the rat's life.

Cécile turned quickly. "Sper—" she began, but she never finished what she was about to say. For as the rat's body toppled forward, his fist came down at last. That great metal gauntlet struck Cécile's skull, and she fell alongside the rat in a heap.

Delphine felt the crushing blow and then her body slammed to the ground. She heard Speranta screaming from behind her. Through glazed eyes, she stared at the rest of the rats. Their leader slain, they turned tail and ran.

She tried to take a breath, but the pain was too great. A mist was rising in front of her eyes. She could see Speranta kneeling down beside her, felt a cool paw on her cheek. Cécile's cheek. Speranta gave a sob of grief.

Then the world slid sideways, turned black and cold . . .

The voice again, wind in the leaves. *"Now you see."*

Delphine slammed back into her own body so hard that she

was thrown against the wall. Tears fell from her eyes, not from the pain, but from what she had just lived through. Crying, she struggled to sit upright.

"You gave your life for her! For all of them!" Sobs ripped through her. The feeling of being Cécile, dying in Speranta's arms . . . it was still so fresh and raw. Then Alexander was kneeling beside her, clasping her paws in his. The warmth of his touch slowly brought her back to the present.

When she could finally breathe again, she gazed up at Cécile's ghost. "But why seal up the whole wing?"

Cécile's voice was fading. It floated to her like a puff of smoke, already disappearing into the air. *"Too much for Speranta to bear."*

Remembering the look on Speranta's face, the anguish in her voice, Delphine understood. She would have never wanted to set paw near the place again. No wonder a whole new entrance to the school had been constructed, this one closed up forever.

Cécile's form was wispy now. *"Find the baby,"* came one last whisper. Then she was gone.

Delphine's cheeks were wet with tears.

Alexander grabbed her by the shoulders. "What baby? What just happened?"

Delphine tried to pull her thoughts together. "I . . . I don't know! I saw how Cécile died. I saw my ancestor, carrying the needle . . . and she was carrying a baby, too. Speranta said . . ." Delphine struggled to recall. "The mouse came from Arc des

Dieux. Something about a château with three trees." She looked up at Alexander. "Does that mean anything to you?"

He shook his head.

Delphine rose. Her mind was racing. She had to find that château.

✳   ✳   ✳

Rolanta Fortencio looked surprised when Delphine and Alexander entered her study. "Back so soon? How goes the search?"

Delphine didn't want to waste any time. "I know where my ancestor came from, before she passed through this school. Somewhere near Arc des Dieux. A château?"

Rolanta blinked. "How did you uncover this information so quickly?"

Delphine had been hoping she wouldn't be asked that question. "Well—"

"A ghost," interjected Alexander. He squared his shoulders. "A ghost showed us where to look."

Oh, no. Delphine hardly dared look back at Rolanta.

But Rolanta's ears had gone white as ash. "Cécile." She said it as a prayer, as a commandment.

Delphine squeaked in disbelief. "You knew that there was a ghost back there?"

"I told you that most of the scribes found the space

unpleasant for any length of time." But she would no longer meet Delphine's eyes.

Unbelievable! That would explain why Rolanta had been in such a hurry to leave them.

"I think Cécile is lonely," Delphine told Rolanta. "Maybe it's worth reopening that part of the school." She paused. "Cécile saved my ancestor's life. I'll never forget that. But now I fear I have brought the same danger to your school. I've already seen rats in town. . . ." She trailed off, unsure of what to say. She had no protection to offer them.

Rolanta rose, taking Delphine's paw. "We can take care of ourselves. As for Cécile . . . I had no idea she wanted company. I always thought she wanted to be left alone." She blinked. "What did you say about a château?"

"Something with three trees, I think?"

"The Château Trois Arbres. It's been there for centuries. Just past Arc des Dieux, where the river curves north and then back east again."

"Then that's where we're going next." Delphine stood tall, refusing to think of how long it might take with winter's icy fingers moving farther south every day.

✳ ✳ ✳

Once more they had little to pack, but once more they were recipients of kindness by their host. Rolanta pressed two thick hooded cloaks on them, lined with dandelion fluff against the cold, as well as a large cloth bag. It was heavy with nutmeats and breads. A little paper packet rested on top.

Delphine could smell what it held. The anise-seed cookies. She looked at Rolanta. "Do you know . . . when Cécile spoke to me, I could smell these. Didn't you say that these cookies are an age-old school tradition?"

Rolanta nodded slowly, her brow wrinkled in thought. "I always wondered why. Perhaps they were Cécile's favorite." She handed over a slim folio of papers. "I almost forgot. A gift for you."

"Thank you." Delphine slipped the folio into the sack alongside the packet of anise-seed cookies. "And thank you for all your kindness. I'm in your debt."

"As I am in yours," Rolanta responded gravely. "You've brought peace to our ancestor. I only hope you can track down your own as well." She clasped Delphine's paws warmly. "I wish you both safe travels."

✳ ✳ ✳

Delphine and Alexander trotted back down Rue Fortencio as it curved around the church like an oxbow.

Alexander reached for the bag. "So what did she give you?" He opened the folio and a gust of wind whisked a sheet of vellum into the air. More sheets threatened to break free.

"Careful!" Delphine dove, snatching the page just in time. She turned it right side up and looked over Rolanta's handwriting. "'This is an old melody from our songbooks,'" she read. "'It is rarely sung nowadays, but I hope this may be of some help on your quest. It is a small token of my gratitude.'" She glanced down at the lyrics that took up the rest of the sheet. "It's about the Threaded!" she squeaked excitedly. She started to read the song aloud:

Tale of the Threaded

Listen, oh listen, I'll tell you a tale,
Of mice who hold magic from ear-tip to tail,
Who travel the land sewing doublet and cloak,
For great lords and ladies, each item bespoke.

These mice called the Threaded, they stitch and they sew,
But the needles they use are from long, long ago.
They can darken the sky, and cast out from sight,
But also bring power and set wrong to right.

"That's fantastic," interrupted Alexander, his paws tucked inside the sleeves of his new hooded cloak against the cold air. "But can we save the rest for later? This wind is positively freezing my tail."

The weather had taken a definite turn for the worse. A chill wind dogged them up the streets to the end of town, where as promised, they found the foot of the path into the forest. They looked at one another, shivering.

"Lead the way, Delfie," Alexander said, wrapping his cloak ever tighter.

✳ ✳ ✳

They weren't ten minutes outside of the city, zigzagging their way up a narrow path through rocks and trees, when a large furry animal stepped out from behind an old oak stump.

A cat.

They froze, nowhere to hide.

Delphine thought of Lucifer back home and prayed that this feline wasn't as cruel. Or at least . . . at first glance, she had thought it was a cat. Now that she was looking at it clearly, she couldn't be quite certain.

Its huge round eyes were golden green, staring unblinkingly at them. Spiky gray fur stuck out in every direction, even from between its toes. The fur was so thick around its ears that she could barely see them. Its mouth hung open, tongue protruding slightly, one fang jutting upward at an odd angle. Whatever it was, it was terrifying.

Beside her, she could hear Alexander reaching for his sword, then cursing when he remembered he'd lost it. She dared not break her gaze with the creature. Its perfectly round eyes, pitch-black in the center, stared back at her. Its tail slowly swept into view, then swept away again, like a metronome keeping time.

Nobody moved.

At the center of the creature's strange flat face was a tiny nose from which snorts and snuffles were coming intermittently. Delphine had thought at first it was snarling, but no attack seemed forthcoming. It was simply standing there, watching them. She began to wonder if this was simply how it sounded when it breathed.

Then it opened its mouth, and Delphine tensed in fear. "Hello," it said, in a nasally, gravelly voice. The tone was oddly friendly.

Delphine cocked her head, trying desperately to catch Alexander's eye without completely looking away from the thing.

It spoke again. "Are you Delphine?"

Delphine and Alexander both jumped a little. She recovered first. "I am," she said carefully. Was this some sort of trap? The rats' doing, perhaps?

"Pleasure to meet you," it said. As it spoke, bits of spittle sprayed randomly. It licked its lips and they both flinched, but it went on, apparently unaware of the significance of the gesture. "I've been waiting for you. Rolanta sent me."

Now Delphine was truly speechless. Rolanta had sent a monster after them?

It grinned, showing far too many teeth. "I'm here to protect you while you're traveling to Château Trees, or whatever it's called. I've been there before. I can show you the path up the banks of the river. It's not easy this time of year for little creatures like you. She thought you might like some extra help."

Delphine managed to gather herself together. "I'm sorry, and you are . . . ?"

"Oh!" It grinned again, drool dripping a little from its crooked fang. "I'm Cornichonne. So lovely to meet you. Both of you." Cornichonne turned the full force of her unwavering golden gaze on Alexander, and he shuddered a little.

Delphine gave him a sharp glance. Then she looked back up at the creature. "Very nice to meet you, too," she replied, trying as hard as she possibly could to stop thinking about the last time Lucifer had caught one of the mice of the château. "How, uh, how did you know who I was?"

Cornichonne squinted her huge eyes as much as she was able. "Not many mice wandering around out here with silver whiskers and a silver needle."

Delphine's paw flew to her face. She had gotten lax about powdering her whiskers with dirt. She would need to be more vigilant. Then she saw that the creature was wearing leather saddlebags, and bulging full, from the sight of them.

Cornichonne noticed Delphine's gaze. "Yiss, she gave me plenty of dried fish in payment for helping you." Delphine's face must have fallen a little, because Cornichonne continued hurriedly. "And mouse foods, too, no doubt. But oh, that delicious fish . . ." Her wide eyes went a little dreamy.

"Y-you eat fish, then?" asked Delphine as politely as she could.

"Of course!" said Cornichonne. "Don't all cats?"

Delphine gulped, suddenly glad she hadn't asked what sort of creature Cornichonne was.

And so Delphine and Alexander gained a new travel companion. A curious sight it would have been to any other passersby to see two mice traveling with a cat. But there was nobody else on the trail that day. It seemed that they were all alone in the autumn forest, and as Delphine thought again of the rats in Parfumoisson she prayed it would stay that way.

the morbier m●●n

Chapter 17

The saddlebags had yielded a curious array of items, presumably what Rolanta thought would best serve travelers during winter. The packet of whisker wax was much appreciated by Alexander, and there were several truly useful items like blankets and bowls. But many things that Delphine would have included in a heartbeat were missing.

"Packed by a shrew who's never actually set paw in a forest," commented Cornichonne, noticing the look of frustration on

Delphine's face. "But we can forage whatever else we need." She started licking one of her front paws.

"Like a cooking pot?" Delphine folded her arms a little petulantly. She felt at once irritated at herself for questioning the shrew's kindness, and afraid of the reality that was looming before them. Living on the road would just get harder as winter began to descend.

The cat shrugged and started in on another paw. "Who knows what we might find?" She sneezed suddenly, spraying Delphine, Alexander, and all the laid-out belongings, before resuming her washing. "'Scuse me."

Delphine and Alexander looked at each other.

"Are you thinking what I am?" she muttered quietly to him.

"Walk *behind* Cornichonne," he whispered, wiping the fine spray of goo from his whiskers. "Though it's still nice having another companion along with us."

"Let's repack the saddlebags for her. It's one thing we can do."

They did walk behind the cat after that, but not only because of the occasional sneezes. Cornichonne could break a path when the branches or grasses were too thick for the mice to easily navigate. And the cat knew her way up and down this river, judging from her familiarity with the path as they traveled.

In the long hours they walked, Delphine told Cornichonne all about her needle, the tapestries, and her quest to unravel the mystery. She spoke of the rats and their terrifying pursuit.

Cornichonne agreed. "You don't want to tangle with rats," she said solemnly. But she was fascinated to learn about Delphine's ancestor who had visited the music school a century ago.

"Who was the baby?" she liked to muse aloud. "Your great-great-grandmother? Your great-great-great-grandmother? But then again, you might not be a direct descendent. I know a cat who inherited his aunt's curly whiskers. Could silver whiskers work the same way?"

Delphine would always have to shrug and say she didn't know. Cornichonne was asking all the same questions she had been turning over in her own head ever since they had left Parfumoisson.

At night Delphine would sit in front of the twigfire with her needle in her paws, trying to connect with the magic. Each time, she could summon the fizzy feeling of the power inside her veins a bit more, but it took an enormous amount of concentration. She longed to move beyond the basic magics that she had mastered so far: lighting a fire, wiping away mud stains, straightening a frizzled whisker. Again and again, she would push hard with the magic, eager to discover just how far she could go. The result was either nothing at all, or clouds of sparkles that collapsed into dust. On one unfortunate evening, she had focused so intently on trying to awaken the needle, it had backfired in her face with a massive silvery explosion. She had found herself sneezing silvery shimmers for days.

But still she continued to practice. Summoning more patience than she had thought she possessed, she began to discover that if she relaxed and let herself fall into the magic, she could make things happen—truly magical things. One afternoon, Delphine noticed a branch of pussywillow hanging low over the path ahead of them. It was as bare as any pussywillow would be in late autumn, and she found herself thinking of how her mother loved the fresh buds every spring. She pictured them, smiling idly, at the same time feeling the silvery tickle running over her paws and through her needle. Then she jerked to attention and saw that the branch was now dotted with tiny green buds. But even as she looked, her attention fully on the sight before her, the feeling faded away. In an instant, the buds had vanished in a mist of silvery sparkles.

She stood stock-still, staring hard at the branch. Had that *really* just happened?

Alexander was at her side, shaking her excitedly. "You did it! You did it!"

She grinned slowly at him. "I guess I did."

✳ ✳ ✳

Cornichonne would sometimes tell jokes in that gravelly whine of hers until both Delphine and Alexander were doubled over laughing, at which point the cat would stop and stare at them sternly. "You have to be quiet in these woods," she would say, drooling on them in the process, which would send them into fits of laughter all over again.

She sang sometimes, too, and one of her tunes always seemed to tickle the back of Delphine's mind. She had never heard it before, but somehow she still *knew* it.

Over hill and over dale,
Through the dappled autumn light,
Comes the hidden silver vale.
Enter if your heart is bright.

In the clouds we mice reside,
Castle floating high above,
Runes will open gateways wide,
Lead you to your heart's true love.

Call, my dear, and I will run
Across the waves to bring you home.
Now I watch the setting sun,
Taste the bitter honeycomb.

"Are you sure that's the last line?" Delphine asked when Cornichonne had finished. "'Bitter honeycomb'?"

"Far as I know," the cat replied.

"Well, I love your voice," Delphine said, for Cornichonne's low crooning was oddly soothing in its monotone quality. "Do all cats sing?"

"I don't think so," responded Cornichonne. She nosed a few large twigs aside so that the mice could pass safely. "But I don't really know what other cats do. They never wanted to spend any time with me. That's why I ended up visiting the music school so much."

That seemed sad to Delphine, even though her newfound appreciation of Cornichonne had done little to curb her fear of the rest of the cat population. But the idea of this sweet creature being ostracized, just because she looked different from the rest; it made Delphine's heart break a little. "That's awful."

"But I never would have met Rolanta otherwise, and come to live in the church, and learned all those songs."

They walked on. "You don't live in the music school?" Delphine asked.

Cornichonne laughed, a cacophonous series of snorts. "Oh, no! How could I fit in there? I live in the human church overhead. But Rolanta comes and visits me, and I listen to them singing every day.

"I help the school, too. I bring them all the seafood they can eat. I'm excellent at fishing." She paused in her stride long enough to extend one paw, claws curving in front of her. "They dry the fish and use it for their meals, but there's plenty left over for provisions whenever I decide to travel."

"So then Rolanta didn't actually pay you to escort us," Delphine said slowly.

"No. I just said that so that you wouldn't think I was strange for showing up there. Rolanta told me about you, and I thought you might want some help. I know what it's like to be lost and alone. She *did* pack the saddlebags. But it was my idea to see if you wanted a guide up the river. Is that strange?" She looked almost nervous.

"No!" Delphine cried, scurrying over to the cat. "I don't think that's strange at all! Honestly, that's one of the most incredibly kind things I've ever heard." She stretched up and managed to pat Cornichonne's chin.

"As kind as when I came along on your adventure?" called Alexander from behind the two of them, but Delphine understood that tone by now.

"Not quite!" she teased, and he laughed.

✳ ✳ ✳

In the evenings, Delphine sometimes pulled out the sheets of lyrics that Rolanta had copied for her. She pored over them by firelight but could make nothing more of them. Now she noted down the lyrics to Cornichonne's song, as well as the other songs she had overheard at the Fortencio Académie, and gazed at them all side by side. Could they all be about the Threaded?

"Do you know any more songs about mice like these?" she asked the cat, showing her the written lyrics.

"Not sure." Cornichonne peered at the sheets, gnawing away on a piece of dried fish. "Are you certain you don't want any of this?"

Delphine shook her head. "We've still got plenty of barley," she said politely. "Thank you, though."

"More for me." Cornichonne smiled and went back to her gnawing.

Delphine went back to examining the lyrics, but if there were any secrets hidden there, they were locked up tight.

One morning when the fog was thick and they were cutting across a harvested wheat field in an oxbow of the river, Cornichonne turned to the mice. "I'm going hunting. You both keep on moving. I'll catch up with you."

Delphine and Alexander were used to this by now, and continued on as Cornichonne disappeared across the wide field. The morning fog felt thick and damp around them. Delphine shivered, then noticed that Alexander was doing the same.

"It's creepy out here," she said softly. "It feels like the trees are watching us."

"That's because it's cold," he replied. "Maybe we should stop and make a fire."

"We need to keep moving."

"You're freezing. I'm freezing. Let's stop."

"No." She kept walking.

Alexander crossed his arms. "You have to stay warm!"

She glared at him over her shoulder. "Shh! You're talking so loudly, the entire forest can hear you."

A low hiss broke through the mists, stopping them both in their tracks.

"Hush!" He put a paw to his lips, but Delphine had already gone silent. They stood stock-still. The sound came again, crawling through the air toward them.

"Look!" Delphine whispered. She pointed at the field before them. The dead grasses were bent in places, crushed. "Are those pawprints? *Rat* prints?"

Delphine reached for her needle as Alexander pulled out the sharpened little stick he had taken to wearing in his sword belt. The field stretched bare on either side of them. There was nowhere to hide.

"Hello, little mice," came a blood-curdling whisper through the mists.

Delphine and Alexander turned frantically side to side, wide-eyed with terror.

"We've been waiting for you." Another voice, sibilant and sneering.

"Show yourselves!" squeaked Alexander. He redoubled his grasp on his little stick-sword.

"All I had to do was catch your scent, little one."

Heart racing, Delphine tightened her grip on the needle, trying to summon the silvery magic. If she could figure out how to disperse the mists . . .

But before she could do anything, a stoat and an ermine emerged in front of them, sly grins on their faces. Delphine and Alexander were trapped.

"Mouse!" called the ermine as she stalked toward Delphine. "Give me that needle!"

"Never!" Delphine cried. "Neither one of us will answer to you!" She pointed her needle toward them, hoping she could summon some dangerous-looking magic.

The ermine laughed tauntingly. "I think you will, little mouse. No one refuses Valentine. And your friend will make a tasty bite for Snurleau here." She licked her lips with a pointed tongue, gazing at Alexander.

Delphine cried out, bringing her needle into the air above her head. Her voice pierced the sky, and a rush of sparks flew from her needle. *It worked!* she thought.

Snurleau hesitated for a moment, but Valentine charged forward. She and Delphine met head-to-head. Valentine drew her dagger, a cruel-looking curve of razor-sharp steel. Delphine brought her needle down like a sword, crashing against the dagger and sending up flashes of sparkling magic. Each blow of the needle caused dark magical burns across Valentine's metal blade.

Alexander ran toward Snurleau. The stoat leapt into action,

slashing with his claws, but Alexander fought valiantly, weaving and stabbing with his stick.

Valentine shook her head and snarled. Delphine snarled back, charging toward her, needle raised. But Valentine slashed with her other paw. Delphine barely managed to dodge, falling hard on the frozen earth. The ermine spread her jaws wide and plunged for the kill.

A streak of gray flashed across the field, heading straight for them. It was Cornichonne. She smashed into the side of Valentine, sending her skidding across the grasses. The ermine pulled herself up as Cornichonne stood protectively over Delphine, fangs bared. Blood dripped in blobs from her jagged fangs to the frozen ground. Her tail lashed madly from side to side, stirring up clouds of ice.

Snurleau scrabbled backward away from the cat, falling over in the process. "What in nutmegs is that?!"

"Coward!" Valentine kicked him, and he leapt back upright. "We're not afraid of you . . . whatever you might be," she snarled at Cornichonne, her voice like oil on silk. "We'll take you all down, one at a time. My blade will see to that."

"Alexander!" Delphine called desperately.

The noblemouse ran to join Delphine between Cornichonne's front legs. The cat made a terrible low growl that neither of them had ever heard before, a sound that would have made their blood run cold if she hadn't been on their side.

Valentine and Snurleau started backing away, but whether

to retreat or regroup, Delphine couldn't tell. Then Cornichonne leapt toward them in a surge, eyes gleaming. Delphine seized the moment and stepped forward, raising her needle again. Focusing her powers, she channeled coils of silvery magic that flew toward the pair, wrapping around their arms and legs like vines.

Their bodies suddenly bound by magic, Valentine and Snurleau cried out in horror. They flailed, breaking through the silvery vines, then turned tail and ran. Cornichonne pursued them, chasing the pair across the field.

Their voices faded as they retreated, arguing as they went. "Midnight'll have our heads!" came Snurleau's faint voice.

"I didn't sign up to fight magic!" was Valentine's reply in the distance. Then they disappeared into the woods on the other side of the field.

The silvery swirls vanished in a flash, and Delphine's whole body suddenly went limp. She swayed, leaning against Alexander.

"Are you hurt?" he cried, holding on to her protectively.

"I don't think so," she said, but she leaned against him for another moment anyway. Then something suddenly occurred to her, and she pulled back to look at him.

"Hang on." She shook her head to clear it. "You can *fight*?"

"Why yes, of course." He looked surprised. "Swordplay is required for all young lords and ladies of the court. Every Tuesday and Saturday on the north lawn."

"No, but you really *do* know how to"—she waved her arm around in the air—"do all that stuff. I always thought your stories were, well . . ."

He looked at her quizzically. "Did I not tell you the tale of when I single-handedly fought off the hawkworms?"

She blinked. "Yes, but . . . well, aren't hawkworms just little green harmless things?"

"Not when they're threatening the safety of the castle croquet garden."

Delphine grinned as he wrapped his arms even tighter around her. She hugged him back, realizing she was grateful for the warmth as well as the company.

The sound of approaching pawfalls made them jump apart. Cornichonne returned, licking black blood from her lips and making awful slurping sounds. Alexander turned away.

"Did you—" Delphine suddenly felt a little faint.

"Oh no, no," said Cornichonne, still slurping happily. "I just caught a weevil on the way back to keep up my strength. I let them lose themselves in the trees. That forest is full of devilthorn. They're going to be pretty unhappy. Still, better for us to get as far away as we can, and in a different direction, just in case they're watching."

They worked their way deeper into the forest, finding a stream, where Cornichonne drank deeply. The mice both refilled their acorn-shell water carriers. Then they all crawled into a makeshift cave created by tree roots and frozen earth.

Cornichonne passed out instantly on a pile of dry leaves, snoring in soft whuffles.

Delphine gazed at the towering trees that flanked the cave. She had been shaking all afternoon, terrified that the enemy had been able to find them so easily. "We're still too exposed here." She let the needle rest in her paws, gazing hard at the entrance and the darkness beyond. If only the branches of the tree hung just a little bit lower . . .

Letting her gaze soften, Delphine imagined the branches, heavy with pine needles, bowing down in front of the cave. The needle tingled in her paws. Slowly, the branches descended in front of them until the cave was completely hidden.

She turned to Alexander and found him gazing at her. She looked away again quickly. "We all need to rest," Delphine said before he could volunteer to take first watch. "This will hide us."

They wedged more dry leaves between Cornichonne and the walls of the cave to keep her warm. Then they dug themselves into the leaves, making two little mouse nests next to the cat.

The wind tore through the trees outside. Soon, snores and sleepy wheezes joined the sound.

But one of the adventurers was still awake, a question turning over and over in her head: Why had an ermine and a stoat been on the hunt for her needle?

Had the danger expanded beyond just the rats?

Interlude

Rien glanced around, double-checking that nobody had followed him down the broad stone hallway. Then he quickly crossed and pulled back a tapestry, knocking at the little door hidden behind it.

Elodie cracked it open a smidge. At the sight of Rien, she flung it wide. "Come in!" she whispered happily.

The forgotten chamber was just one of many that dotted the corridors. It never ceased to amaze Rien how many rooms had simply stopped being used over the hundreds of years that the mice had lived here—rooms that were then hidden away as furniture was moved, tapestries were rehung, and entire wings were abandoned.

This was one of his favorites. The cozy space shared a wall with one of the many kitchen chimneys, ensuring it was always warm, even on the wintriest of days. The window looked out over the misty rocks to the swiftly flowing river and the endless forest beyond. Elodie had even smuggled in a few pieces of furniture over the years. It was their own special place.

Now he settled happily into one of the old overstuffed armchairs, tucking his paws up under him. "I brought some morsels," he said, offering the little sack to her.

She took it, pouring its contents out onto a tray. "Cheese! And walnut meats! How did you manage to smuggle this out of the kitchen?"

"I was careful."

Elodie shot him a look. "But what if you had been caught? It's not worth it, risking your safety for something like this. Besides, I have enough to eat. You're the one who's always going hungry."

His face must have fallen, for she gently touched his paw. "It was very kind of you," she added. "But next time, you should bring something that won't put you at such a risk. Maybe some beautiful stones from the river, like the ones we used to play with? We could line them up along the windowsills. It would be so pretty."

Rien nodded. "I'd love to." He was already thinking about which of his favorite little river stones he would add to their cozy hideaway.

They sat and chatted, laughing over silly stories, trading tidbits of *gossip, talking about everything and nothing, as they had since they were little children. Rien ate voraciously, and Elodie kept encouraging him to have just one more piece, just one more crumble, even pushing her own plate of food over to him. Years had passed since they had first met, and although they had both grown up, he was still so small, nearly as small as a mouse.*

Rien, ever optimistic, told her all about the sunset he had seen and how gloriously the clouds had glowed. He shared how he had seen a mealworm eat its way into a loaf of bread and never come out the other side, and she laughed until she cried.

"But who ate the loaf?" she asked, still laughing, and he shrugged, grinning back.

"There are some mice upstairs who I wouldn't mind seeing eat a meal-worm," she giggled. "Especially the old monsieur. Always lecturing us on the dangers of our magic. 'Keep your heart pure when you cast. Don't meddle in life and death. Never touch time.' *He's so dull. Why would I want to do any of those things anyway? Turning leaves into butterflies is so much more fun!"*

Rien was always awed at how she spoke so casually of her talents. Her lovely face glowed with joy as she described the butterflies she had made just that morning, and he gazed at her. He thought he had never seen anyone so beautiful, so full of life.

Elodie noticed the glazed expression in his eyes. She stopped talking. "Now I'm boring you."

"Never!"

She reached out and squeezed his paw.

He squeezed back.

Upstairs, the chosen mice were busy with the duties and responsibilities of their birthright. Downstairs, the servants gossiped among themselves. But in their secret room, Rien and Elodie sat together, rat and mouse, best friends across two worlds.

Chapter 18

Travel along the river was slow, even with a cat to lead
the way. And each day, the sun rose a little later and
disappeared a little sooner, making daylight travel more and
more of a luxury. Delphine and Alexander did their best to
stretch the barley grains from the saddlebags into as many
meals as possible, but all too soon it was back to roots and nuts.
They spent hours digging in the hardened ground, finding only

dried-up fragments of roots. Other foragers had already been there, leaving little in their wake.

It grew colder every night as well. With the frigid air seeping into their bones even through their cloaks, they found themselves edging closer to Cornichonne each night. After a few nights, Delphine was snuggling into the cat's neck, and Alexander took to curling up between Cornichonne's paws. Delphine knew her old self would have been amazed that she was sleeping so close to a feline.

During the day, Delphine and Alexander struggled with being exhausted and half freezing most of the time. It didn't help that Cornichonne seemed to always be in good spirits, no matter the circumstances. She would sometimes disappear for a few hours and come back licking fresh fish scales off her paws, looking most satisfied.

"I wish we could fish for acorns," Alexander always said when she returned, only half joking. Their food supplies were running dangerously low.

One morning, Delphine couldn't get up. Her body had nothing left to give. She suspected that Alexander wasn't faring much better, though he tried to put on a brave face.

"What's wrong?" asked Cornichonne, sniffing her gently. Her warm breath felt oddly comforting.

"Cornichonne, I can't . . . I'm just so tired," Delphine admitted, trying to hold back tears. She hated to say it, had fought for days against admitting it, but could deny it no longer.

"Oh," Cornichonne said sadly. "It's a lot of walking for you little creatures, I suppose."

Delphine nodded, too weary to reply.

Cornichonne gazed at her, clearly pondering something. Then she lay down on her belly next to Delphine, paws stretched forward. "Would you want to . . . ride on my back?"

Delphine stared at her in disbelief. *Break the animal code? A cat giving a ride to a mouse?* She couldn't imagine such a thing.

When Delphine didn't respond, Cornichonne bowed her head. "I didn't mean to insult you," she said awkwardly. "I just thought—"

"No!" Delphine struggled to stand, then slowly approached Cornichonne. She wrapped her arms around Cornichonne's neck as best she could. It was the tiniest of hugs to the cat, but Delphine meant it with every bone in her body. "I . . ." Delphine struggled to find words. "You would do that for me?"

Cornichonne nodded solemnly. "You've worked so hard to get this far. Maybe I can help you, just a little bit." She looked at Alexander. "Both of you."

Alexander approached and bowed low. "You do us a great kindness, Lady Cornichonne. I think you to be one of the kindest denizens of all this kingdom." Even in his now-ragged garments, he looked more handsome than Delphine had ever seen him.

Impulsively, Delphine kissed Cornichonne's moist nose. "Thank you."

They rolled the blankets and tucked them under the saddle-bag straps to form impromptu saddles. Then, one by one, they climbed awkwardly onto her back. Cornichonne walked to and fro as Delphine and Alexander got their bearings. Within minutes they were at ease, rolling with the cat's sinuous gait as she walked, holding on to her thick fur like reins. Cornichonne put out their twigfire with a few backward kicks of dirt, and they were on their way again.

As Cornichonne walked, Delphine was lulled into a gentle state of reflection. She let her mind wander, observing the trees they passed and the clouds up above. But her thoughts always returned to the needle. Why had it been left with her? What was the use of it? She knitted her brow, trying desperately to see a pattern. She thought of what her mother had said, about finding the knot in order to unravel the mystery.

She knew now that her needle had been one of the Threaded's, long ago. Somehow, it had been stolen by a mouse who was pursued by rats, just as she was pursued now. But where had the needle been for the last hundred years?

She couldn't see any answers in that direction. She tried another angle. The needles were spoken of in all the tales of the Threaded as the symbol of their power. Obviously, the needle held magic even greater than she could summon. But why was she able to tap into it at all? She thought back to that night in the boat, then even further back to the monastery. The shimmering walls.

Could Father Guillaume have been one of the Threaded, and somehow given her the keys to unlock the magic of her needle? No, that was absurd. The Threaded had been mice, not badgers, and they had all disappeared a century ago.

But no matter *why* she had awakened the needle those few times, the bigger question seemed to be: *How?* If she wasn't able to control it, to wield it properly, she would have no hope of protecting herself if the rats caught up to them.

And she had a sinking suspicion that they would. The kingdom was only so big, and there were only so many places to hide. She couldn't live on the run forever. Sooner or later, she would have to face them and defend the needle, or die trying.

And your parents? whispered a little voice in the back of her head. *Your birth parents? You're still no closer to knowing why they gave you up.*

"Maybe I never *will* know!" snapped Delphine aloud, tired of longing for answers that were always out of reach.

Alexander jerked out of a doze behind her. "Did you say something?"

"It's nothing, Alexander," she said without turning. "Go back to sleep."

The air was starting to feel damp. In another moment, it began to drizzle. The shower of droplets quickly turned into heavy rain, which became a downpour. Cornichonne continued onward, apparently unbothered, but within minutes the two mice on her back were thoroughly drenched.

"It's a s-solid wall of w-water," Alexander managed to get out between chattering teeth.

It felt as though they were underneath a never-ending water-fall. "It l-looks like glass," he continued unhappily. "We're riding th-through liquid g-glass." Even bitterly cold, he couldn't stop himself from continuing a one-sided conversation.

But Delphine suddenly pictured what he had said. *Liquid glass.* If it were liquid . . . could she make it solid? She pushed back her hood, heedless of the torrent of water that instantly poured down on her head, and stared hard at the rain. Someone had made shoes of glass. Could she make glass out of rain?

Delphine squeezed her eyes shut, imagining the droplets clinging together to form a smooth solid sheet of glass above their heads. The needle began to tingle in her paws.

The rain began to lessen. Her eyes snapped open. Overhead, the droplets streamed outward on either side of them, running down to the ground. There was a faint shimmer in the air.

Delphine reached out one tentative paw to touch the shimmer. It felt solid. She laughed in delight.

"Alexander!" She turned to look at him behind her, and the shimmer faded for a moment as she lost her concentration.

Oops. She faced forward again, letting the needle rest in her paws and keeping her mind calm. The shimmer strengthened once more. Alexander slapped her on the back excitedly and she grinned, but kept focusing. The glass sheet above them was holding.

$$\text{✳ ✳ ✳}$$

After that, practicing with the needle didn't get easier, but it did become more rewarding. Several times she was nearly able to make a pebble rise into the air. The sparkles would gather around it, and it would begin to wobble slowly upward, but then fall back to the ground. When she sighed, Alexander would always come to her side.

"That's so much more than you could do before! Delfie! Don't give up!"

And she didn't. It helped to have his cheerful support in those moments of doubt.

On the other hand, she could have done without his endless questions about how the needle and the magic worked.

They were resting after lunch one day, Cornichonne dozing next to them as Delphine reattached a button that had fallen off Alexander's jacket, when he started up with the questions again.

"I don't understand how you do it," mused Alexander. "Sometimes you make gestures, but you said that other times, you just imagine what you want the magic to do and it happens?"

Delphine shrugged, unwilling to admit that she was just as baffled as he was by the needle. She focused on the task at hand, twisting a weedy stalk of grass so that it could slip through the buttonholes.

"Hand me your jacket," she said.

"And then yesterday," he went on, his jacket still dangling

from his paw, "you couldn't do anything but make the needle fizz and crackle all afternoon, like a spitting fire built out of wet wood."

"True," she said shortly, reaching for his jacket. She deftly wove the thin stalk of grass back and forth through the fabric to attach the button.

"So I can't help but wonder," he continued, "what would happen if you tried something really big?"

She threw the finished garment on the ground. "Oh, *thank you*, Alexander. Thank you for that excellent and thoughtful tip. It hadn't occurred to me to try 'something big,' as you so cleverly call it. I've just been hoping to do really *small* magic. That was in fact my goal." She stood up and grabbed her needle from where it was leaning against a branch. She couldn't bear to even look at him for another moment.

Alexander turned to Cornichonne, a confused look on his face. "Well, shouldn't she try that?"

Cornichonne awoke briefly to answer with a whuffly snuff.

Stomping into the forest until she found a little clearing, Delphine sat down in a huff, skirts billowing around her. She leaned her head against one paw. Didn't Alexander see that she *was* trying?

After a few minutes, a courtly nose poked through the grass, followed by Alexander's narrow face and elegant ears. "Delfie?" he said quietly.

"What?" She knew she was being sullen, but she couldn't help it.

He crossed and sat beside her. "I believe in you. I just don't know if you always believe in yourself. That's all I was saying. I believe you can do big things."

Delphine looked at him, feeling irritation melt into guilt and endearment. She took his paw. "Thank you."

They sat for a moment. Far away, a lone blackbird cried out, piercing the chilly afternoon air. Then, realizing the moment had gone a smidge too long, they hastily dropped paws, scrambling to stand and avoiding each other's gaze.

"Shall we head back and find Cornichonne?" Delphine asked briskly.

"Indubitably."

the sainte-maure m●●n

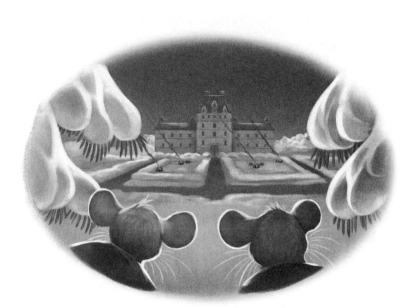

Chapter 19

The three travelers finally reached the Château Trois Arbres, its pointed roof looming in the chilly air. As they drew closer, they could see smoke rising from the many chimneys. Alexander breathed deeply. "I can almost smell the chestnuts roasting!" Delphine licked her lips at the thought.

It was lucky that their pawsteps had been silent on the barren ground, because as they drew closer they began to see that they were not the only ones who had come to the château. Multiple twigfires flickered faintly between the tree trunks of the wintry forest. Dark, ominous figures moved to and fro slowly, as if keeping watch.

"I have a bad feeling about this," whispered Alexander to Delphine.

"You're not the only one," she replied.

"I'll scout it out," Cornichonne announced, staring at the château. She slipped into the twilight and was soon swallowed up by the trees.

The mice waited, nervous, until the cat reemerged just as silently. "Rats. Troops and troops of them." Cornichonne's usually golden eyes were huge and dark. "They've set up little camps all the way around the château."

Delphine's blood ran cold. They hadn't seen a hint of the rats since leaving Parfumoisson. How had they known that Delphine would be coming here?

She dropped low and began crawling slowly as far forward as she dared. When she had reached the last copse of trees before the grounds that surrounded the château, she halted. Now that Delphine knew the dark figures were rats, she could make out their shapes more clearly. Cornichonne was right. It wasn't only that there were a lot of them, but they were also spread out across the entire area.

Delphine ground her teeth, tiptoeing back to rejoin the others.

"We're going to have to try to sneak past them," she whispered, ignoring Alexander's less-than-thrilled expression at this plan. "We'll wait until it's dark. The moon is young, so the night will be quite black. If we go quietly, perhaps we can tiptoe right between their camps and get into the château without them ever knowing.

"Cornichonne, can you wait here in the woods? Once we're inside . . ." She hesitated. She had no way of knowing what sort of mice lived within the château, or if Cornichonne would be welcomed. "We'll figure it out once we get there," she said finally. "But we won't forget about you."

Cornichonne nodded, unconcerned. "I'll do some more spider hunting."

Crawling along the frozen ground once more, Delphine beckoned Alexander to follow. Dead grass tickled her nose, and she suppressed a sneeze. When they could see the full spread of the front grounds, she settled herself onto a chunk of dry wood. Alexander squeezed in next to her.

They waited for it to get dark, peering at the rat patrols and memorizing their patterns. When night had finished falling, they watched as the rat that had been patrolling directly between them and the château went wandering over to a nearby camp, presumably for a break.

Then they made their way down the brushy slope as quietly as they could.

Under the dim light of the crescent-thin moon, the twig-fires glowed in the lees of low hedgerows planted in decorative patterns. They must have been designed as fanciful labyrinths for lordmice and ladymice. Now they were pocked with groups of bloodthirsty rats.

All was still as Delphine and Alexander tiptoed along the route they had identified, moving closer and closer to the château and its glowing windows. Then Delphine heard the faint sounds of rats laughing and talking. She crossed her toes and tail that it was too dark for her and Alexander to be spotted. The sounds faded and they were alone once more.

When they were nearly at the outer ring of walls, Delphine took stock of their surroundings. Nothing stirred to the left, to the right. Delphine turned her gaze forward once more . . . and found herself staring straight into the cruel red eyes of a massive rat.

It loomed before them, larger than any rat Delphine had ever seen, blotting out the light from all the château windows. One of its hind legs was gone, replaced with a wooden stump. Its rank breath blew hot against her ears.

"Mouse scum!" The rat swiped with its yellowed claws, nearly catching her in its grasp. "How dare you trespass in our camps!"

The rat's claws grazed her and she tumbled, falling head over paws. She managed to leap up and veer to the left, but another rat emerged from the bushes. Alexander backed up until he stood next to Delphine, shakily pointing his stick-sword at the rats closing in from the other side. Jaw trembling, Delphine reached back to take hold of her needle. She wasn't going to be captured—or killed—without a fight. But her paw met thin air. Her needle was gone. The sheath was empty.

Delphine spun madly, danger forgotten, thinking only of one thing—she had to keep the needle out of the rats' clutches.

"Alexander!" she squeaked, fear rising in her throat. "Do you see my . . . ?" She gestured at the sheath, realizing even in her panic that the rats might not yet have noticed her needle was missing. He glanced around wildly.

The rats were calling back and forth now, alerting the others. "Intruder mice!" she could hear them growl. "Crossing onto our side, are they? We'll show 'em what happens when rules aren't obeyed!"

The rat in front of them moved a half step toward her and light from the windows streamed down once more. On the gravel of the path where he stood, a gleam of silver caught Delphine's eye.

The needle must have been knocked from its sheath when the rat grazed her. Now as he shifted his weight, his wooden stump of a leg came down on it, pinning it to the ground. Had he seen it?

One glance at his face told Delphine that the rat had no idea of the treasure that now lay trapped beneath him. She hesitated. Was it really worth risking her life for this object that was still a mystery?

The answer was clear—the needle was all she had to unlock her past. It was the only thing that connected her to her birth parents. Not to mention, it held untold powers. She couldn't let it fall into the paws of evildoers.

Before she could lose her nerve, Delphine lowered her head and charged straight toward the beastly rat.

Surprise spilled across his face, beady eyes widening. "Hey!" he bellowed. "What do you think yer playing at?"

She eyeballed the space between his belly and the ground as she ran, thinking of the narrow passageways in the walls of Château Desjardins. Maybe it was lucky that this rat was so tall.

His eyes narrowed, lips peeling back until the full length of his fangs showed gleaming and wet. "That's how it is, is it?" he snarled. "Gonna spit you for Midnight myself, then."

She could hear Alexander calling her name, but she didn't turn back. The instant before she reached the rat, Delphine dropped to all fours, still running. The rat's paws slammed together in the place where she had been a split second earlier, but she was already skidding through his legs. As she passed, she swiped with her claws at the flesh just above his wooden stump. He yelped, pulling his leg away from her attack.

Success! The needle momentarily uncovered, Delphine managed to snatch it up with her paw. She kept running away from the rat as he reeled from her unexpected attack.

"Delphine!" Alexander sounded closer. She glanced up, still clutching her needle so tightly that her knuckles were white. He dashed toward her, pointing as he ran. "Look!"

Delphine turned to see a solid wall of soldier mice pouring

out of the château, clutching weapons and running straight at them. Her heart soared.

She leapt up and began to sprint alongside Alexander toward the mice and the château wall. As they grew closer, she noticed that the soldiers' swords and halberds were raised, but they were coming no farther. It seemed as if an invisible line existed at the edge of the innermost garden ring.

Delphine and Alexander reached the mice, who separated to let them through. Then the ranks of soldiers gathered together again, gazing menacingly at the rats.

"Back to your side, rats," shouted one soldier mouse. She swung her sword to emphasize the point. "You know the rule."

The rats grumbled and snarled but slowly backed away. Delphine couldn't believe it. Just threatening the rats with a rule—that was all it had taken?

As the rats dispersed back to their camps, the mice turned on Delphine and Alexander, staring intently. They had not lowered their weapons. Delphine gulped as she and Alexander found themselves backed up against a solid stone wall. Four of the soldiers loomed in front of them. Were they in league with the rats? *Impossible.*

Delphine and Alexander braced themselves, but the mice didn't lay a paw on them or attempt to disarm them. They gestured brusquely for Alexander and Delphine to walk toward the front entrance of the château. More confused and afraid than ever, Delphine and Alexander complied with their silent escorts.

Inside the front hall of the château, they were greeted by a wigged and beribboned footmouse in full livery. He bowed low. "Lady Delphine," he intoned. "Lord Alexander. Welcome to the Château Trois Arbres."

What knavery was this? Delphine redoubled her grip on her needle, but was surprised to hear Alexander slipping his stick-sword into his belt. She glanced over to see that his face had split into a huge grin. "Bertrand! We are at your service." He clapped the footmouse on the back.

"You old so-and-so!" continued Alexander heartily. "What on earth are you doing here?"

"I'd be more fitted to ask you that selfsame question!" came the reply.

"Wait a minute," put in Delphine, now utterly lost. "Alexander—you *know* him? And you . . ." She turned on the footmouse who was apparently named Bertrand. "Aren't you at all concerned that this château is entirely surrounded by rats? For that matter, why are the soldiers spending their time taking us prisoner instead of fighting off the enemy?"

Alexander rested a gentle paw on top of hers, and she slowly lowered her needle. "Delphine," he said, "Bertrand has been a loyal footmouse of the castle for as long as I can remember. Whatever brings him here can only be good news."

Mice from the castle were here at the château? Had they known she would be headed here in search of answers about the needle? Delphine leaned against Alexander, feeling light-headed.

"Bertrand! What a shock this must all be to Lady Delphine." Alexander put his arm around her. "We have traveled far and are weary and in need of nourishment." He gazed down at her again. "We are safe here, my lady. The soldiers of the castle who brought us inside simply didn't recognize me. But can you blame them?" And with a wry smile, he gestured at his bedraggled travel clothes and mud-caked paws.

The chambers they were led to were sumptuous, but Delphine barely noticed until she'd gotten several cups of steaming hot barley tea in her, along with two servings of apple-jam cakes and nearly an entire brussels sprout. The serving mice bustled about all the while, bringing in clean garments and fresh linens. One of the serving mice looked unaccountably familiar to Delphine, but she couldn't quite place her.

Alexander hovered around Delphine, introducing her to everyone he recognized, which only made Delphine's head spin more.

"Let her rest first," said a motherly hedgehog who had appointed herself as Delphine's keeper. She gently fussed over her, combing her whiskers and picking the bits of dirt from her wounded paws before cleaning and bandaging them. "You both are in a right state. The difference is, you know who we are. She doesn't."

After Delphine ate, she dozed. When she next opened her

eyes, she found sun streaming through the windows. Alexander was watching from his seat across the room. She struggled to sit up, and he came to her assistance.

"You slept for quite a while," he said.

Delphine nodded. "I didn't mean to, but—"

He cut her off gently. "You needed it."

"Thank you for staying with me," she said. She looked around more carefully at her surroundings. On either side of the canopy bed, the drapes were tied back with rich gold threads. Elderberry logs burned fragrantly on the hearth. Above stood a marble mantel cunningly supported by the rooks of a human chess set. "Where are we? I thought you didn't know this place. But you know the residents?"

Alexander seesawed his head. "Not the residents. The guests. I know the footmouse who met us at the door, and a few of the servants who came to care for us last night."

"How?"

"From court. The royal retinue is here because they accompany the princess whenever she travels."

"The . . . princess? She's here, too?" Delphine gasped. Then she recalled the serving mouse she had recognized. It had been Ysabeau, Princess Petits-Oiseaux's pawmaid.

Alexander nodded, ears pink with enthusiasm. "And we've arrived at the most perfect time. The Winterberry Ball is mere days away!"

But attending a ball was the last thing on her mind. She had unwittingly brought grave danger straight to Princess Petits-Oiseaux's doorstep.

"Hold on," Delphine said, waving her paws in the air to try to get his attention as Alexander wondered aloud whether he could borrow proper attire from another lord for the ball. "What about the mice who captured us?"

"They weren't capturing us. They were escorting us to safety. They were as surprised as we were that the rats attacked."

"But why would anyone be surprised to see rats attack? Isn't that what rats do?"

"No, no, those rats out there are the 'mis-rule.'" Seeing the blank expression on Delphine's face, Alexander continued. "The rat guard that tracks the movement of the mouse royalty. It's been like this for a hundred years. Something to do with the cease-war. Whenever a member of the royal family travels out into the kingdom, the rats of the castle send a whole troop to trail along and keep an eye on where the royals are going and what they're doing. So the royals bring along a whole battalion of mouse warriors to 'protect' themselves from the rats. But they never fight. It's all just for show."

Delphine thought that she would never understand the ways of the royal world. But she had more immediate concerns.

"They *did* fight, Alexander. The rats tried to kill us."

"Well . . . we didn't arrive with the royal caravan. So I

suppose we were considered fair game? I've never traveled with the royals before. I don't actually know exactly how the mis-rule guard works."

Delphine bit her lip, thinking intently. "I don't think they knew who we were," she said finally. "If they had recognized me, they wouldn't have stopped when they did."

"Good point." Alexander attempted to stifle a yawn.

"Your turn to rest," she said. "Just like keeping watch at our forest camps, right?"

He smiled, not bothering to protest.

"There." She pointed to a sofa just on the other side of the room. "Lie down and sleep. I mean it. And we'll . . ." She leapt up, suddenly realizing what had been gnawing at the back of her mind. "Cornichonne!"

But Alexander had already curled up on the sofa. "She's fine. I snuck her into the cellar. She was very . . ." And he was out, snoring into his whiskers.

Delphine rose and walked to the window. Her heart sank as she gazed down on the sward surrounding the château. The rats' little campfires flickered ominously, strewn like hot coals in every direction.

Chapter 20

Delphine wandered through the château halls, gazing around in awe. It was fascinating, she thought, how the entire château had been built entirely by mice, to the scale of mice, *for* mice! She had never seen anything like it. She had spent her whole life in a human-size château, where the rooms *inside* the walls were mouse-size, but the walls themselves were scaled to humans. Here, everything—the staircases, the mantelpieces, the cornices, all of it—was sized for her.

She was welcomed into the princess's quarters by her paw-maid, Ysabeau. Princess Petits-Oiseaux was perched on the settee in front of her dressing table. Bearnois, her pet bumble-bee, was buzzing in lazy circles nearby. The princess spotted Delphine and a lovely smile ran across her face.

"Ma chérie!" The princess rose elegantly, stretching out both of her paws. Delphine approached and took them gladly, bending into a curtsey. But the princess pulled her upright and into a warm embrace.

"I am so pleased to see you, my dear. When I learned that you had disappeared on the same night the rats had crossed into the castle . . . I grew most worried! And nobody seemed to know a thing." The princess's eyes were damp, and Delphine found herself touched that the princess could care so deeply about just one of her many subjects in such a large kingdom.

"I'm fine," Delphine hastened to reassure her. "And Alexander has been at my side the whole time. Lord Alexander, that is."

The princess nodded. "I was so glad to learn that he was also safe. We've been worried for months. Some feared that the rats had carried him back across into the Forbidden Wing when they retreated."

"Then the rest of the castle was unharmed?"

"All perfectly safe and sound," Princess Petits-Oiseaux told her. "We castle residents don't let a little thing like rats stop us. Not even when we're traveling. Although I do hate to be away at such a time . . . did you hear? The human prince has been searching high and low for his mystery princess! It's all terribly exciting." She took a step back and looked Delphine over. "My pawmaids have been taking care of you, I see."

Delphine nodded. Cleaned, scrubbed, beribboned, cosseted, corseted, and finally topped with several splashes of eau de géranium, Delphine was feeling more elegant than she had since the whole adventure had begun. There was just one thing. "I don't quite know how you manage to be so comfortable in these court garments, Your Highness," she admitted. Delphine had had to borrow a whole new set of clothes to replace the ones that had practically fallen apart when the maids tried to wash them. It was only then that she realized just how loose-fitting and comfortable her country garments had been.

The princess let out a peal of laughter that tinkled like a bell. At the sound, Bearnois floated toward her. His huge dark eyes regarded Delphine softly. "You are such a dear!" she said. "Whoever said that these were *comfortable*? Oh no, no, no, there's nothing whatsoever comfortable about court clothes."

"Then why wear them? Why not wear knee ribbons and heeled shoes like the lords? Surely those give greater freedom of movement."

"Even less, my dear, even less. You think that we ladies suffer for our fashions; you have no idea how the lords are stifled and laced into their finery. It's all the way of the court, you see."

"Your whiskers, though!" The princess gazed admiringly.

"You know I loved them when they were gray . . . but this silver is so striking. However did you manage it?"

Delphine, flattered that the princess remembered her gray whiskers, related the moment she had held the needle in her paws under the light of the full moon.

The princess's eyes grew wide. "So it was almost as if your whiskers had been coated in a sort of tarnish, too. And when the needle's tarnish was affected, the other was as well?"

Delphine hadn't even thought of that. The rumor around the kingdom had always been that the princess was clever, and Delphine quite agreed.

She nodded. "How true!" Then she paused. "I'm sorry, Your Royal Highness, I just still can't believe that you're *here*."

The princess laughed again. "I can't believe that *you're* here!" she returned. "Imagine, as I'm standing at the window last night, what do I see but two mice heading straight into the rats' camps? And then learning that the rats had engaged in an attack?!" Her voice hardened and Delphine saw her paws clench. "The castle rats have *never* attacked, not in a hundred years. They've harried and hounded us, following us across the kingdom and back, upholding this ridiculous mis-rule of theirs. But they've always kept an understanding with my guards. Neither side attacks the other, and thereby all remains in balance.

"At least—" Princess Petits-Oiseaux stared out through the window at a flat gray sky. "At least until now. Perhaps peace is coming to an end. We must hope not, but it seems the winds may be changing." She turned back to Delphine. "My little dressmaker." She smiled. "You have been on quite an adventure. You must tell me all about it."

And so Delphine shared the tale of the past few months.

The princess listened in rapt silence, and when Delphine finally finished, she shook her head in amazement. "And you ended up here, at the Château Trois Arbres, only days after my arrival. Incredible!" She clapped her paws together. "Clearly it is too dangerous for you to travel without an escort. And although I'm sure you wish desperately to return home at once, unfortunately I cannot spare a single guard. We travel lightly when we can."

Princess Petits-Oiseaux's definition of "light travel" seemed very different from Delphine's. But she politely replied, "I'm pleased to be here with you, my princess. And actually, I'm looking forward to exploring the château to see if I can uncover any clues about my ancestor or the needle."

The princess tapped one paw against her lips, contemplating. "Now how could the rats have possibly guessed you would be coming here?"

"I don't think they knew who I was when they attacked," Delphine explained. "Now that I know about the mis-rule, I think that they just happened to see two mice who had no business being on their side of the camps. A bit of easy prey for rats with nothing else to do but sit and watch a château for days."

"Yes, I see." The princess nodded slowly, her powdered

whiskers bouncing lightly as she did so. "Well, you are safe now. And you are welcome to whatever the Château Trois Arbres can offer. I hope it holds the answers you seek."

✳ ✳ ✳

The task of looking for these answers quickly became overwhelming to Delphine. The château seemed to contain an endless number of rooms, suites, chambers, antechambers, closets, foyers, backways, and other similar spaces tucked into every corner. And she had thought that little Château Desjardins was full of winding passages and hidden rooms!

After hours of wandering, she stumbled upon a grand, high-ceilinged hallway lined with full-length windows down one side and massive tapestries down the other. The tall windows allowed plenty of daylight to stream in so that viewers could enjoy the delicate craftsmanship of the tapestries.

She walked along slowly, studying the tapestries one by one. They told the story of the mouse family that built this château, generation by generation. The oldest ancestors were dressed in styles Delphine barely recognized. Then her heart soared as she noticed mice in the tapestries who were wielding giant needles to create magic and sew beautiful garments. So there were tapestries of the Threaded here, too!

Delphine returned to the hallway the next day and spent all afternoon staring at the tapestries. She examined every stitch.

She copied down the lists of names embroidered around the edges of one where Threaded mice stood front and center. *Maydeline, Ertice, Arcon, Elodie, Pierrette, Martine, Claudien, Gielle.* She even sketched out some of the design elements of their garments, the embroidery details around their cuffs or on their tail covers in the winter tapestries. But nothing was revealed.

Deciding to take another avenue, Delphine spent the next few days questioning the regular staff of the château, becoming a well-intentioned but often overfriendly visitor to the kitchens and the other servants' areas. Did they know anything about a mouse with silver whiskers visiting the château a hundred years ago? What about stories of a human-size needle, carried by a guest? Had their ancestors worked at the château, and if so, had they ever told tales of such things? She frequented the wings where the family who owned the château now lived and questioned them, too, as much as she dared. She feared to take advantage of the kindness that Princess Petits-Oiseaux had extended her, but she was desperate to unravel the mystery.

Sadly, no matter whom she asked or where she looked, there were absolutely no clues of any kind. Nobody had ever heard any old tales from the previous generations of a silver-whiskered mouse visiting the château, carrying one of the Threaded's needles.

Delphine's growing disappointment did not go unnoticed. One day, Princess Petits-Oiseaux summoned her back to her chambers. Taking in Delphine's drooping whiskers and melancholy eyes, she announced brightly, "My little seamstress! I can't tell you how pleased I am to have you here. I was just trying on the gown I had planned to wear for the Winterberry Ball, and it simply doesn't flatter me one bit. Ysabeau, please have it removed." She nodded to her pawmaid, who swiftly collected the mass of tulle hanging in Princess Petits-Oiseaux's dressing room.

"I hang my hopes upon you," the princess continued gravely. "The ball is in just three days. Can it be done?"

"Why, yes, of course, my princess!" It was just what Delphine needed—an achievable project. With new energy in her step, Delphine scampered out of the princess's suite to begin tracking down whatever sewing tools and materials might be available throughout the château.

She spent many hours over the next few days in Princess Petits-Oiseaux's chambers, and each day her spirits rose a bit more as she poured her talents into her latest creation. The princess smiled at her all the while, and said nothing.

The needle was coming in handy, too. When Delphine needed gold-braid trim, she found she could use the magic to coax a strand of golden thread to knot itself into an intricate pattern. And when she could only locate cream tulle for the skirt—not the snowy white she'd imagined—the needle gave that little fizzy jump in her paws that she was coming to recognize. She gazed down at it, then back at the bolt of fabric. Well, why not? She knew how dyes worked. If she could just reverse the process . . . And so, Delphine focused her energy, picturing the cream hue lightening bit by bit. As Delphine's ears tingled with the effort, the color of the tulle faded until it glowed a perfect white.

Delphine laughed aloud. It was, of course, nothing more than a parlor trick. She wouldn't ever be able to save a life by changing fabric colors. But as a seamstress—how useful this magic was becoming! And her understanding of just how gifted the Threaded had been was growing every day.

Her time filled with these endeavours, Delphine barely saw Alexander. She wondered sometimes what he was doing with his days, but she couldn't bring herself to worry too much. He was back in his element, after all, surrounded by courtly folks and doubtless doing courtly things.

When she *did* spot him one night at a formal dinner, she asked quietly after Cornichonne. He whispered that the cat was just fine, and very happy down in the cellars.

"She loves it down there, actually," Alexander told her. "So many little tunnel bugs to hunt." But guilt gnawed at Delphine. Cornichonne had helped them get to the château safely so that she could search for clues, and Delphine had nothing to show for it.

✳ ✳ ✳

As the Winterberry Ball drew closer, the pitch in the château grew frenzied. Chambers were aired out and prepared for guests, the grand ballroom was decorated in lavish detail, and even the hall of tapestries received constant foot traffic as staff and servants bustled in every direction.

Delphine found herself thinking more and more of her mother back home, preparing for the winter holidays with the rest of the mice of Château Desjardins. When she was little, she had always imagined that the holiday celebrations at the castle were much more exciting than their dull country dinners. But now that she was actually in the midst of a royal celebration, she found herself missing her old life. She pictured all the mice of the château gathered together, laughing and celebrating as they split the traditional chestnut-cake.

The evening before the Winterberry Ball, Delphine carefully slipped the finished gown over the princess's head and pulled it down to lace the bodice, not trusting even the pawmaids for the final fitting. The main overskirt had been designed to look like a single holly leaf, wrapped around and cleverly pinned in place by a decorative clasp. Underneath, piles and piles of shimmering white tulle shifted as the princess moved, giving the impression of light dappling onto the snow.

Delphine sighed contentedly. It was perfect. The princess turned to see herself in the glass and squeaked. "Absolutely exquisite!" she said, nose pink with happiness. "But what about you? What will you wear?"

"I wasn't planning on attending," Delphine admitted.

"Nonsense!" The princess waved a paw. "You could use some merriment. It won't hurt for you to take one night off. Please. Find something in my closet—anything at all."

Delphine smiled, grateful for her newfound friend's kindness.

$$* \quad * \quad *$$

The night of the ball, Delphine dressed with a flutter of excitement in her stomach. She had chosen a ruby-brocade gown embroidered with rich gold thread. The ruffled neckline set off her narrow shoulders to beautiful effect, while the broad skirts were full enough to pass muster for an evening formal ball. Delphine couldn't imagine being away from her needle for that long, so she cobbled together a gold leather case that she could strap to her back.

The guests had been arriving all day, carefully escorted past the rats as custom dictated. Now they were lining up outside of the grand-ballroom doors, whispering and squeaking excitedly to one another. All the servants ran to and fro, completing the final touches.

Delphine had offered to stay with Princess Petits-Oiseaux to ensure that her outfit was displayed to perfection as the guests filed in, but the princess declined.

"Don't be silly!" she laughed. "Enter with Alexander like

a proper guest! Seeing the ballroom as you make your grand entrance is half the fun!"

And in fact, when the doors swung open and Delphine gazed upon the wonderland that lay before her, she had to agree. The ballroom had been transformed into a glistening fantasy of ice and snow. Princess Petits-Oiseaux stood in the center in front of a pine sapling that towered above, bowing under the weight of the glass icicles, crystal snowflakes, and spun-sugar candy canes that hung from every branch.

Two by two, the guests entered and were presented to the princess. Royal footmice stood at either side of the doors, announcing the names in their fullest baritones.

"Lord and Lady von Vertisme Muffley-Puffley of the Muffley-Puffley estate!"

"Lady Terafine Chouette and Lady Doyenne Moins-Soleil!"

As they waited in line, Alexander kept telling Delphine how wonderful she looked, using his most chivalrous tones. Maybe it was the magic of the evening, but Delphine found herself appreciating his compliments. She even fluttered her eyelashes a little.

"Duke Blancmange aux Cerises Vertes and Duchess Pantoufle-Courgette!"

But as Delphine and Alexander drew nearer to the front, her enthusiasm slowly congealed into nervousness, then dread. She had no title. She had no name, not that anyone would know.

Alexander noticed her growing consternation. "What's wrong?" he asked quietly.

She looked away, not able to meet his gaze. "Nothing," she said, hoping to brush it aside. "Isn't this a lovely evening?" She tried to smile once more, but her lip quivered. To her horror, she could feel tears gathering. She clutched at the little reticule Princess Petits-Oiseaux had lent her.

"Your introduction," Alexander said gently as they moved another step closer to the footmice asking for names and titles. "It's your introduction, isn't it?"

She shook her head vigorously. If only he would stop looking at her.

"Don't worry, Delfie." He drew himself up and gently took her paw, placing it on his forearm. "I'll handle it."

Oddly enough, she believed him.

They stepped up to the footmice. "Your names?" intoned the senior-most.

Alexander cleared his throat. "Lady Delphine Silverthread Desjardins, Needle-Bearer of the Desjardins estates, honored guest of Her Royal Highness Princess Petits-Oiseaux."

The footmouse blinked a little but didn't lose his composure. "And . . . your name?"

It had to be the first time that Alexander had ever forgotten to provide his *own* title. Delphine giggled, unable to help herself. He flashed her a grin of his own. "I'm just Lord Alexander de Soucy Perrault," he stated offhandedly. "*She's* the honored guest."

The footmice stepped to either side of the doors. As Delphine and Alexander moved forward, their names were announced.

"Impressive!" she said under her breath to Alexander as they descended the stairs.

"What, your title? Or his delivery of it?" he said back, equally sotto voce.

"Both."

"You deserve every word," he said.

Delphine's heart leapt in her chest unexpectedly, and her ears flamed. She tried to compose herself, looking around for any sort of distraction. "Ah! Dessert! Shall we?" She dragged him toward tables sagging under the weight of trays, dishes, and tureens filled with all the candied sweets, roasted nuts, sugared trifles, and other holiday delicacies that the kitchen had fever-ishly turned out over the last few days.

They sampled one bite of each treat, and then they went back for seconds of all the best ones. Alexander suggested a few times that perhaps they might like to dance. But each time, Delphine found a way to change the subject. She couldn't bear to admit to Alexander that she had never learned any of the courtly dance routines that were being performed by the guests. Her former nervousness was beginning to return.

It didn't help that other guests kept approaching. "Ah, the honored guest of Princess Petits-Oiseaux!" they would say, bowing or curtseying low. Delphine couldn't help but wonder if they were secretly making fun of her.

"They aren't," Alexander had assured her after she'd finally admitted why she was looking so uncomfortable. "They simply want to meet the honored guest." But Delphine was starting to wish that Alexander hadn't been quite so enthusiastic when he had dreamt up her title. She was sweating under the heavy gown, and her head hurt from all the conversations happening on top of one another. She had never heard so many mice all talking at the same time.

A slow waltz began, and Alexander extended his paw ceremonially. "You must surely join me for this one," he said to her, quirking his eyebrow in that Alexander-ish way that she had come to recognize. But it was all too much. The ladymice around her, stepping onto the dance floor with light, easy movements. The gentlemice, equally full of grace. And all of them believing her to be someone she wasn't.

"I . . ." She backed away from Alexander. "I just need to get some fresh air." He looked at her quizzically and she managed a wan smile. "I'll be right back."

Delphine walked back to the ballroom's main doors as calmly as she could, just in case he was watching. Once in the hall, she turned tail and ran blindly, not knowing where she was headed, the needle case banging against her back. She let the hot tears finally fall from her eyes. She didn't belong here. She didn't belong anywhere.

Chapter 21

When Delphine could no longer hear the festive strains of the ball, she finally slowed. The gown, heavy with embroidery and gold thread, was making it hard to move, and her paws were sore in the thin silk slippers. She walked quietly, miserably, staring out through the tall glass windows. The Sainte-Maure moon was full, its light peeking through the heavy clouds that blanketed the night sky. She pawed at her tears, forgetting about the delicate lace handkerchief tucked into her reticule.

After a while, Delphine found herself in the hallway of tapestries. She tiptoed down the hall, her silk slippers silent on the marble floor. In the darkness, the embroidered colors seemed to glow. She thought of the walls in the monastery. It felt so long ago.

She had nearly reached her favorite tapestry, the one that portrayed three of the Threaded riding on snail mounts, when she suddenly caught sight of a dark figure sitting on one of the chairs.

Delphine froze. She had been certain that every guest, every servant, was in the grand ballroom enjoying the festivities. Who, then, was this?

"Hello?" she called out, her voice quavering a little. She could make out the silhouette of a bent head in a mobcap, full skirts tucked neatly. Then the figure leaned out of the shadows, and Delphine saw the face of an ancient mouse, one whom she had never seen before. Her whiskers were trimmed short in the fashion of half a century earlier, and her garments reflected the same era, though everything about her was immaculate. Her eyes twinkled beneath the ruffled edge of her mobcap—a mobcap, Delphine could now see, made from the finest Venetian silk and trimmed with hand-tatted lace.

"Child," the mouse said gently. "Why are you not at the party?"

Delphine found her manners, and curtseyed politely. "My lady," she began, for this mouse was clearly a lady of one of the kingdom's noble families. "I was tired and came for some fresh air."

This was met with a chuckle. "You were tired . . . so you walked across three wings and up four flights of stairs?" The bright eyes seemed to see straight into Delphine's heart. "You were tired not in body, but in soul, I think?"

Delphine took a deep breath that turned into a ragged half sob. Despite all the troubles that had been weighing upon her for months—fleeing for her life, fearing for her mother's safety, nearly starving and freezing—in this moment, the shame and humiliation she had felt in the ballroom as an outsider somehow overwhelmed everything else. She could stay strong in the face of near death, but she was crumpling like a leaf under social pressure. It was so silly! She took another raggedy breath, trying to calm herself. "I don't know how to be one of them."

"Nor do I." The elderly noblemouse gazed into space thoughtfully. "I *am* one of them, and I still do not know how to be one." She gave Delphine a wry wink. Delphine couldn't help but laugh shakily through her tears.

"I am Philomène," the noblemouse said. "And you are?"

"Delphine, my lady." She gave another curtsey. "It's a pleasure to meet you, Lady Philomène."

The noblemouse sniffed. "I gave up on the pretense of titles long ago. The more titles you carry with you, the more masks you find yourself hiding behind. You must call me Philomène, and I shall call you Delphine in return, if that meets with your approval."

"Of course." Delphine found herself already fond of this curious old mouse, sitting ramrod straight in the hall of tapestries. "*You* didn't want to go to the Winterberry Ball?"

Philomène waved her paw in the air. "I saw the beautifully decorated ballroom." She glanced sideways at Delphine and gave a tiny smirk. "I snuck past the officious footmice who were insisting upon announcing every single guest—what a tedious, tiresome folly *that* is!—and I enjoyed the tastiest of the sweetmeats."

Delphine let out a proper laugh, and it echoed through the hall. She clapped her paws over her mouth, but Philomène joined her, guffawing even louder. The sound danced against the glass windowpanes.

"And then I came here to enjoy the view of the moon," continued Philomène. "I have no interest in putting on airs anymore."

Delphine sat down impulsively on the floor in front of Philomène's chair, putting down her needle in its sheath beside her. "I wouldn't even know what airs to put on," she said. "I'm not from anywhere. I don't even know who I really am." A fresh tear slid down onto one of her whiskers. It hung like a glimmering dewdrop, and Delphine turned her head away in shame.

Philomène produced a handkerchief and passed it over. Then she turned respectfully to gaze at the tapestries, giving Delphine time to compose herself.

"I never tire of these weavings," Philomène said when Delphine had stopped sniffling. "And I still dream of the Threaded. It was my favorite tale as a pinkie mouse. *'They lived in a castle in the clouds.'* That's how it always began. *'Once upon a time, the Threaded lived in a castle in the clouds.'*"

"I've never heard that line," said Delphine, her curiosity piqued.

Philomène smiled. "It's all here in this hall with us." The ancient mouse gestured expansively with one wizened paw. "Read the tapestries, dear. The stories of the Threaded are woven into them."

"Then whoever made the tapestries . . . had to know the stories somehow." Delphine found herself drawn into Philomène's words. This was far more interesting than feeling sorry for herself.

"Oh yes. There was a workshop of weavers in the heart of the north's largest city, Montrenasse-sur-Terre. I remember visiting it when I was very young. It was the same workshop that made all of the finest tapestries for all the finest homes in the kingdom."

"Then . . ." The wheels were turning in Delphine's head. "If I went to that workshop, maybe I could find more tapestries of the Threaded. More stories of them, woven into the fabric. More clues?"

Philomène watched her silently.

"It's worth a try," said Delphine, hoping to convince herself. She looked back at Philomène. "And what was that you said, about them living in the clouds? The story you heard when you were little . . . how did it go?"

Philomène shook her head. "That was so long ago, my dear. I only remember fragments now—how they plucked rubies from thin air and stitched them together into real roses. How they traveled the kingdom, sewing for those who were kind and loving. They brought magic into the world around them. They were the heroes of their time."

She and Delphine sat quietly, looking at the tapestries. Then Philomène spoke again, half to herself. "I like to think of what they might be doing today, if Midnight hadn't destroyed them."

Delphine's eyes widened. "Midnight?" she squeaked. "The rat outside . . . he said something about Midnight!"

Philomène turned her gaze back to Delphine. "Oh yes. That was always how the tale ended. A terrible rat who called himself King Midnight managed to gain entry to their sanctuary. He killed every last one of them—and every mouse in league with them—in an effort to harness their magic. But he failed. And that was the end of the Threaded."

Delphine sat breathless and horrified. "I've never heard that ending," she finally said. "I'd always heard that they just disappeared and would someday return."

The elderly mouse sighed, shifting on the chair. Her skirts rustled softly. "Fairy tales have a way of getting softened over the years. The most violent parts are sanded away, the story made safer for little ones."

"But . . ." Delphine's mind was racing. "What about Midnight?"

Philomène waved one bony paw. "Another part of the tale that's been revised for being too frightening, I imagine. However, the name King Midnight is still whispered in dark places by evil creatures. That title has been passed down from rat leader to rat leader, each one striving toward the goal of the original King Midnight—to take over the kingdom and destroy all of mousekind."

"So the current King Midnight? He's the leader?" pressed Delphine. She leapt up and began pacing in front of the windows, the drama of the ballroom entirely forgotten. The elder mouse's words echoed in her mind: *He killed every last one of them—and every mouse in league with them.*

Perhaps it was the fact that her emotions were still so raw; perhaps it was the image of the innocent Threaded, slaughtered by the first Midnight and his minions, that sprang to mind; perhaps it was the knowledge that her ancestor mouse would not have been spared. Delphine began to shake with rage.

"Monster!" she cried, slamming her fist against the frame of one of the tall windows. The glass panes rattled under the force of her blow. She could feel the terror that her ancestor must have felt, running for her life, her baby in her arms. And the needle that she carried . . .

Delphine turned and snatched up the needle from where it lay on the thick carpet. At her touch, the metal sizzled with a sudden burst of energy. She stared down with fury at the troops of rats in their encampments below. Hot tears pricked at her eyes.

"How could you kill them?" she screamed. She knew that they couldn't hear her, but she was beyond caring. The needle shook wildly in her paws, sharp silver lines of magic flashing into life in every direction. Overhead, the clouds parted. A cascade of bright white moonlight fell down through the window, pooling around her in the hallway of tapestries.

Philomène was at her side, her gentle touch on Delphine's wrist. "Hush, darling," she said, but Delphine was too far gone. She thrust the needle up toward the moon with both paws.

She cried out wordlessly, all her anger and loss and fear spilling from her in an uncontrollable flood. Jagged spines of lightning streaked up and outward, smashing through the glass panes, reaching angrily into the air. Silvery-blue energy swirled around her like a tornado. Her whiskers sparked at the tips with unleashed magic.

And on the needle, the last of the dull gray pall turned to mist and vanished, leaving behind the true silver, and a line of clear, glowing symbols.

Commandant Robeaux shifted uncomfortably on the frosty ground and stared at the dark shape of the Château Trois Arbres with undisguised irritation. He'd been in a foul mood for months, ever since that needle had slipped through his paws. And now they were on the road yet again, sleeping in mud and gnawing on dried meat, just so that the absurd rule of mis-rule could be upheld. Conditions were miserable, and it was anyone's guess when the mouse princess would decide to head out to her next destination, or where that might be. The paltry campfire flickered meagerly, emitting little light and even less heat.

"Puce!" He jabbed the rat sitting nearest to him. "Get me another flagon of whatever you call this disgusting beverage!"

Puce dragged himself upright and headed across the embankment toward their supply wagons, complaining loudly as he went. Commandant Robeaux was making a mental note to clap him in irons whenever they finally got back to the castle, when a crash of glass caught his attention. His gaze shot upward.

There at a broken château window stood the figure of a mouse. Lightning crackled around her—strange blue lightning that hurt his eyes. And in her paw, glowing silver in the night . . .

The needle! He leapt up. *It's here?*

"Troops!" he roared. He could hardly believe it, but he had gotten another chance. And he would not squander it. "The era of mis-rule is over! We have only one duty now!" He drew his sword and sprinted toward the château, the other rats falling in behind him as they heard his cry.

"Attack!"

Chapter 22

Delphine charged down the stairs, skirts gathered up in one fist. She ran straight into Alexander. Paws flailing, they both tumbled to the floor in a heap.

Delphine struggled to get up, but the masses of skirts, bustles, panniers, and underpinnings that she was wearing made it impossible. He put out his paw and she grabbed it, hauling herself upright. Ugly silver spatters of magic were flying haphazardly off the needle in arcs, landing on the hall rugs and burning tiny holes. She moved to run past him.

"Delphine! Wait! I've been looking everywhere for you. You disappeared from the ball, and now I find you storming through the château hallways with your needle spraying magic in every direction! What on earth is going on?" He grabbed her free paw.

Delphine's eyes blazed. "I'm going to stop all those rats." She brandished her needle like a weapon. "I'll do whatever it takes."

"Those—? Outside?" He pointed in the general direction of the rat encampments, and she tried to yank her paw away. "Delphine. *Delphine!* I don't know what's gotten into you, but you can't go out there. They'd kill you, but also . . . you just said you'd do *'whatever it takes'*? You're not that kind of mouse!" He stared hard at her, entreaty filling his eyes. "You wouldn't do that, not without a reason."

She knew he was right, but the anger still bubbled inside her. "I *do* have a reason. They killed the Threaded. And they killed my ancestor, too."

"*They* did? No, they—"

"Their ancestors, Alexander." She pulled her paw out of his grasp.

"You don't know that."

"Don't defend them!" But her blind rage was fading, and the uneven sputters from the needle were fading with it. The sparking slowed and then stopped.

She sighed angrily. "I figured out who it is that wants to kill me. It's some rat named Midnight. He's the descendent of the rats who killed my . . . great-great-great-whatever ancestor. Now I just have to find out why he wants to kill *me*."

Alexander pulled her close to him. "Don't go out there. Please."

Her anger flared again. "Get off me!" She shoved him and he stumbled backward. Hurt flashed in his eyes, and she felt suddenly ashamed. "I have to do this," she pleaded, as much to herself as to him. "It's the only—"

A crash from the other end of the hallway interrupted her. They could hear glass shattering and wood splintering, metal clanging against metal. Then the terrible screams of mice, and the snarls of rats on the attack.

A nasally growl cut through the bedlam. "Find that needle!"

Delphine snapped back to reality, her ears white. "We have to hide!" She dashed off, Alexander chasing behind her. They sprinted through the first door they found.

"There!" Alexander pointed at a massive armoire. They clambered inside, Delphine's skirts filling the tiny space, and managed to pull the door shut just in time. They could hear the rats thundering down the hallway, slamming against the walls and shredding the wallpaper with their claws as they went.

"Curse the treaty!" came the same growling voice. "Kill them all, kill every mouse in this place until you find that needle! Kill every mouse in the *kingdom*! The treaty is ended!" A filthy cheer sounded as the rats continued to tear along the hall.

The words cut through Delphine like a knife. The fire that had been ignited inside her turned cold. The rats had broken the treaty, all because of her. She stared straight ahead, nose twitching. "They're going to kill everyone," she finally said. It was not a question.

"The royal guard will—"

She cut him off. "They're all at the ball. They have no weapons." She thought she might cry but her eyes remained terribly, horribly dry. She shook her head. "Alexander, I have to save them. It's my responsibility, and mine alone."

Pushing the armoire door open, she clambered down. "I'm going to draw them away from here. I have to make sure they see me leaving. And then—" A lump caught in her throat. She turned away so that he couldn't see her expression. "And then I don't know what I'll do. I won't give in, but . . ."

Alexander followed, wrapping his arms around her. This time she didn't push him away. "I'll help. Please. Let me help."

She closed her eyes, then nodded. "Follow me."

$$* \quad * \quad *$$

The servants' stairway to the cellars was dark and dusty, but at least it was free of rats. Delphine clutched her needle anyway. Alexander had found a rat dagger in one of the hallways they had already passed through. He held it in front of him like a sword.

They moved as quickly as they could, spurred on by the horrible sounds of fighting that were coming from the floors above them.

The air in the cellars was freezing cold and heavy with the odor of ancient mildew. Broken furniture and discarded goods were scattered everywhere.

"Cornichonne!" Delphine called quietly. The word echoed over and over down the tunnels that stretched away from them, disappearing into the blackness.

She shivered, grabbing a thick curtain from a nearby stack of discarded burgundy velvet draperies and wrapping it around herself like a cloak. Better. After a moment, she took a second one and threw it to Alexander. "It'll be cold out there."

Before Delphine could call a second time, a shape appeared out of the depths of the cellar tunnels: Cornichonne, drooling happily at the sight of Delphine, her fur rumpled in messy tufts. She was covered in dust and cobwebs.

Delphine threw her arms around the cat's neck. "I've missed you so. And I'm sorry to say, I need your help."

Cornichonne twitched her funny little ears. "Anything for you."

The air outside was even colder than Delphine had feared. A bitter wind tore through their fancy garments. They clutched lengths of velvet around themselves as protection against the biting cold as Delphine outlined her plan. If only there had been time to change their clothes, time to put on sensible traveling garments . . . but every moment spent in the château meant the potential end of another innocent mouse.

At the corner of the château, she turned to Cornichonne. "You're certain you can get there before us, even if you go the long way around?" The cat nodded. They waved good-bye to her and she melted into the edge of the woods. Then they turned to survey the now-empty sward that they would have to cross.

"She'll be there," Alexander assured Delphine.

Delphine took a deep breath. "I know. Are you ready?"

"After you." He didn't say *my lady*, but Delphine heard it anyway. Before she could lose her nerve, she stepped out into the open. The light from the château windows fell fully upon her. Needle clenched tightly, she raised it above her head, focusing on channeling the moonlight. Silvery shimmers cascaded down, sparkling on the frozen ground.

"Rats of Midnight!" she cried as loudly as she could. "Is this what you seek?"

Delphine watched as one evil face appeared at a window, then another, and another. No longer attacking the mice inside, they were all staring at her.

"Come on!" cried Alexander behind her.

She stood for another moment, until there could be no doubt in their minds that she held the magic needle. Then they began to surge through the windows, throwing themselves from the second and third floors, each determined to have the honor of capturing the prize their king sought.

Delphine turned and sprinted as fast as she could toward the trees.

Snurleau slunk into the throne room, limping a little on his left paw. King Midnight was pacing again. At the sight of the stoat, he stopped, then crossed to his throne. He sank down onto the seat like a pool of oily pitch coming to rest at the bottom of a metal bowl.

"Yes?" he said very softly. He clicked his long, raggedy claws on one protruding arm of the chair. *Click. Click. Click.*

"Your Worship . . ." *Click.* "I mean, Your Kingliness . . ." *Click.* "We were on the mouse's path, but . . ." *Click. Click.*

"Well . . ." Snurleau hesitated, then looked around at the guards that flanked him. "We lost her."

Silence.

The stoat wormed his way to the foot of King Midnight's throne and pressed himself down onto the floor. "Valentine left me, Your Highness. Abandoned me. I was all alone. I did my best, but . . ."

King Midnight dragged one claw across the throne's metal surface, gouging a ragged line. A horrid, high screech shattered the air, and Snurleau winced. "So . . . the needle is gone. Again."

"Y-yes." Snurleau eyed the guards again. "But I have a plan."

"You?" King Midnight rose so slowly that Snurleau could barely see him move. He closed in, bit by bit, a snake sliding toward its prey. "And what, dare I ask . . . is this masterful plan?"

Snurleau twisted his tail between his paws. "We'll set a trap."

"A . . . trap?" Midnight's voice was dangerously quiet. The guards began to back away.

But Snurleau babbled on. "We can lure her in—"

Midnight cut him off. "Stand up." He gestured with one long claw.

"Why?" But Snurleau rose, uneasy.

"So I can see the look in your eyes when you die." Midnight slashed with his claws and Snurleau crumpled to the floor in a heap. The king turned away.

"I need better spies. More talented . . ."

A gurgling sound from behind him caught his attention. He spun around. Snurleau was rising once more, breath rasping unevenly. He pulled out a dagger that had been hidden beneath his cloak and threw himself at Midnight with his last ounce of energy. Snurleau's dagger sank straight into Midnight's chest, piercing his heart.

Midnight stumbled backward. The dagger was buried so deep in his flesh, only the hilt could be seen.

"Fiend!" gasped Snurleau, his breath coming short. "I'm taking you with me!" But then the sneer fell from his face.

King Midnight was laughing.

With one lazy paw, Midnight reached up and pulled the dagger out of his chest, inch by slow inch, until the blade was free once more. As Snurleau watched in horror, the gash in Midnight's chest began to close, the flesh knitting together, until in another moment, there was nothing left but yet another scar.

Snurleau tried to scream, but his breath had left him.

Midnight shifted the dagger in his paw. He knelt down in front of Snurleau, still smiling.

"Nothing can kill me, little stoat," he whispered. "I have magic in my veins."

He brought the dagger down.

Chapter 23

Paws slipping on pine needles, the two mice dashed up the hill toward the edge of the forest. The rats were closing in quickly, but Delphine and Alexander still had a head start. As long as they kept going . . . as long as Cornichonne was there . . .

Alexander yelped as his paw slipped on a rock and he stumbled, falling backward. From behind, Delphine shoved him back upright, panting with the effort. They reached the trees, dodging between the dead branches on the ground, heading toward the log where they had parted ways with Cornichonne when they had first arrived.

"Almost there!" Alexander gasped.

But as soon as they reached the log, they saw that a key component of their plan was missing. No Cornichonne. The clearing was empty.

Delphine's heart rose to her mouth in terror. She could hear the rats among the trees now, baying for blood. "She has to be here!"

They skidded to a halt, frantically looking around. "Can we hold them back; can we stop—?" Delphine started even though she knew the answer.

Then, like a beacon of hope, a flash of gray fur appeared in the trees. Cornichonne was running straight through the hordes of rats. She slowed as she neared the log, and Delphine realized she wasn't going to stop. It was the coach at the castle all over again.

"Jump!" she screamed at Alexander, and they both leapt as the cat raced past, barely landing on her back. They scrabbled wildly to hang on to her fur. The trees blurred around them as Cornichonne sprinted, and they left the clearing and the rats behind.

Cornichonne raced in the dark, the icy wind buffeting all three of them until they were half-frozen. Finally, when they were certain they had lost the rats, she slowed to a walk and stopped. She was still panting, whiskers caked with frozen drool, tongue hanging half out of her mouth. Delphine and Alexander slid off her back, stiff and sore from the long ride. But they were all alive, and they were together.

They managed to find a hollowed-out tree stump, and gathered armloads of dead leaves to build a nest big enough for the three of them. Wind howled through the dead branches overhead.

Delphine tried to apologize for dragging them along with her, but Alexander put his nose into the air indignantly.

"I take offense at your implication, my lady," he began in his most courtly tones. "I have chosen to come on this quest with you. And I believe I speak for Lady Cornichonne as well."

Delphine laughed. It felt good.

"We stand alongside you to help you solve this mystery, track down the truth of your ancestor, and claim your birthright . . . whatever that might be."

Delphine was about to respond in equally pompous tones, make a joke about the quest. But then the faces of the innocent mice at the château swam up before her eyes.

"It's not about me anymore," she found herself responding.

Alexander blinked. "What do you mean?"

"If the treaty is truly broken, then every resident of this kingdom is in danger. Those rats will do the same thing they did at the château, town by town, home by home, until they find me. I can't let that happen."

Alexander fell silent.

Delphine continued, "I have to find him. Midnight. And I have to end this."

✳   ✳   ✳

As soon as the pale sun peeked above the horizon, it was time to go. *Keep one step ahead of the rats,* thought Delphine. *Keep moving toward Midnight and the truth.*

When they emerged from the tree hollow, they saw that a lush winter snow had fallen while they'd slept. The world was hidden under a pale blanket. Ice crystals hung heavy on the last grasses of autumn, bending the stalks toward the ground with their weight. It seemed as if the magic of the needle had passed across the land and left a thick coat of silvery white in its wake.

Delphine gazed at Alexander in his emerald formal wear and his makeshift burgundy velvet cloak. "You're going to stand out like a sore paw in all this snow." She looked down at her own ruby gown and burgundy wrap. "We both are."

She pursed her lips thoughtfully, then pulled out her needle. "Luckily, I've been practicing. . . ."

With a wave of her needle, the colorful dyes drained from their clothing, soaking into the snow in bright puddles around them. Nothing was left but the natural creams and whites of the fabrics used to make the garments.

Alexander's mouth fell open. "When did you learn how to do *that?*"

She winked, sliding her needle back into its sheath. "Perfect."

She and Alexander climbed onto Cornichonne's back and settled themselves in for a long ride, their now-white velvet cloaks wrapped up tightly.

"Let's go, Cornichonne," she said huskily.

Hunched over against the biting wind, they headed into the snow. Winter loomed before them. Delphine's silver whiskers gleamed in the first rays of sun coming over the horizon.

It was time for the little dressmaker mouse to mend her crumbling world.

The End of Book One

ALYSSA MOON grew up in the Pacific Northwest, which explains her undying enthusiasm for rainy weather. She does her best writing in tea shops, independent bookstores, and at home under her grapefruit tree. She lives in Southern California with Picklepop (the "real" Cornichonne), and with three other cats who are a little grumpy at the fact they weren't also given roles in this book. *Delphine and the Silver Needle* is her debut novel.

ACKNOWLEDGMENTS

Words can't express my appreciation to my wonderful editors, Brittany Rubiano and Eric Geron. Thank you both for believing in Delphine from the very start, and being willing to use up all those red pens editing draft after draft. A big thank-you also to everyone at Disney Publishing Worldwide for bringing Delphine's story to the page, and for making the book so beautiful in the process.

Thank you from the bottom of my heart to my parents. My father always kept a drawer full of blank paper for us to write and draw on when inspiration struck, and my mother always encouraged us to check out as many books from the library as we could carry. We didn't have bookcases built into our home; as a child, it seemed to me that our home was built *around* bookcases and the books within them. For that, I am eternally grateful.

Lastly, so much love to my grandmother Jane Elizabeth, who always spoke more gracefully and sincerely than anyone else I've ever known. You told the best stories of all.